Romance Unbound Publishing

presents

Claimed by Two Masters

BDSM Connections
Book Three

Claire Thompson

Edited by
Donna Fisk
Jae Ashley

Cover Art by Mayhem Cover Creations
Fine Line Edit by Gabriella Wolek

Print ISBN 978-1542440660

CHAPTER 1

"Hey, Steve, check out that girl over there. I haven't seen her around before, have you?"

Steve Hartman turned to see whom Zach Wilder, his best friend and scene partner, was referring to. They had just arrived at Hardcore, Portland's best underground BDSM club, after too long a hiatus. From his vantage point, he could see the girl in profile as she leaned forward on the long sofa set against the wall, her elbows resting on her knees, her chin cupped in her hands. In her mid to late twenties, she wore a low-cut dress that showed some very alluring cleavage.

She was pretty, with large eyes and a small, upturned nose. Her hair was pulled back from her face, and from what Steve could see in the dim light of the BDSM basement club, it appeared to be red.

Her expression was a curious mixture of both horror and longing as she stared at the whipping scene occurring in front of her. Following her avid gaze, Steve recognized Harry and Maryanne, a longtime couple in the scene who were regulars at Hardcore.

That particular scene station contained a St. Andrew's cross set on a raised dais, so it was possible to see the action over the heads of the gathered crowd that stood in a semicircle around the pair. Maryanne, naked and bound to the cross, let out a sudden howl of pain.

Steve flicked his gaze back to the girl, who had brought her hands to her mouth, her eyes wide with what seemed to be a kind of thrilled terror.

After a moment, she sat back, her body relaxing, her hands falling away from her face. Her tongue appeared on her lower lip, a dreamy expression now moving over her features.

Looking back to the scene, Steve saw that Harry had dropped his whip. He was stroking Maryanne's hair, his mouth close to her ear.

His eyes returning to the girl on the couch, Steve said, "I haven't seen her at Hardcore either, but I definitely like what I see."

"Me, too," Zach agreed enthusiastically. "She doesn't seem to be with anyone. How about we go say hi?"

"Sounds like a plan," Steve agreed.

They walked toward the long, low couch where the girl sat alone. She didn't appear to notice them as they approached, her gaze still fixed intently on the scene before her. Harry had resumed the whipping and Maryanne was moaning in a low, sexy way that begged for more.

"Hey there," Zach said, smiling down at the new girl. "Is there room for us to join you?"

"What?" The girl tore her gaze from the scene long enough to glance at Zach and Steve. "I'm sorry, yes, of course." Her long, wavy red hair was pulled back from her face and clipped at the nape of her neck with a wide silver barrette. Her shoulders were bare, save for the black spaghetti straps of her dress. Steve instantly imagined the red welts he could paint across her milky-white, flawless skin.

She started to scoot from her perch in the center of the couch, but before she could move, Zach and Steve took seats on either side of her. "We haven't seen you around before," Zach said with a friendly smile. "Is this your first time at Hardcore?"

"Yes. First time," she replied. "Is it always like this? I mean"—she waved toward the whipping station, the scene now winding down as Harry helped his sub from the cross, his arm around her shoulders—"so *intense*?"

"Oh, yeah," Zach said with a grin. "And even more intense if you go to one of the private scene rooms." He extended his large hand toward the girl. "I'm Zach Wilder. Welcome to Hardcore, Portland's premiere underground BDSM club."

"Shea O'Connor," she replied, placing her hand briefly in his.

"And this is my good friend, Steve Hartman." Zach nodded toward Steve.

Shea turned toward him, and Steve took her soft, small hand in his, keeping it there as he said, "Nice to meet you, Shea. I don't see a collar. Are you owned?"

"Am I...what?" She pulled her hand away. "Oh! No, no. I'm here alone. I'm not, um, owned." Her eyes were a vivid blue. The bridge of her nose was dusted with a sprinkling of freckles. Her mouth was small but her lower lip was full and sensual. A flush of color had risen in her cheeks, and she looked down suddenly at her lap.

"I sense you're new to the scene?" Steve suggested, watching her closely.

The color deepened in her cheeks as she lifted her head to meet his gaze. Instead of answering his question, she said, "I'm quite familiar with the dynamics of BDSM," her tone suddenly more formal, more in control. "I'm what you would call an observer of human behavior. I've always been intrigued by the concept of masochism and erotic submission. The whole idea of someone voluntarily allowing another person to subjugate and control them—that they'd willingly bare their throat in submission to the stronger member of the pack, like wolves in the wild"—she shuddered—"I'm both fascinated and repelled that this continues to play out in civilized society."

Ah, Steve thought, amused. *So that's how she plays it.* He had run into her type before—the kind of woman who had trouble reconciling her feminist, hyper-intellectualized take on the world with her more primal, sexually submissive and masochistic desires.

He decided to meet her on her own terms. "I've also made something of a study of BDSM from an intellectual standpoint. But in my ten years in the scene, I've found that intellect will only take you so far. You can watch a dozen demonstrations on proper whipping techniques and listen to lectures about how to flow with the erotic pain, but I can guarantee you you'll learn more from that first cracking stroke of leather or a hard palm against your bare ass than a month's worth of study and research. To really understand dominance and submission, even from a scientific point of view, you need to experience it firsthand."

He could see he had her attention. Her lips had parted slightly and her pupils were dilated. She wrapped her arms around herself in a protective gesture and turned away from him.

Zach, waiting on her other side, took over with a friendly smile. "You know what they say"—he placed his hand lightly on her thigh—"a good spanking is worth a thousand words."

Sensing they might be moving too fast, Steve made an effort to dial things back. "Of course, if you just want to watch your first time out, that's entirely understandable. Some people here never scene. They just move from station to station, watching."

"That's true," Zach agreed, letting his hand fall away from Shea's thigh. "It's important, especially when you're just starting out, to find the right partner. If and when you're ready, you should know that Steve and I are experienced trainers. We'd be happy to initiate you, if you like. Maybe just start out with a light spanking, and see where we go from there."

"A light spanking," Shea said somewhat breathlessly, her eyes widening. "Gosh. I don't know. I mean, I've never…" She trailed off, looking down.

Steve noted her nipples poking against the black fabric of her dress and the flush of color that hadn't faded from her cheeks. She was definitely interested, but uncertain.

He leaned back, returning his gaze to Harry and Maryanne. "No pressure, Shea. It's entirely your call."

She nodded, seemingly reassured as she, too, focused again on the whipping scene still being enacted in front of them.

Taking Steve's cue, Zach, too, settled back against the couch cushions. If Shea was like most subs, she would be doing her own work now—watering the seed of an idea Zach had planted in her brain with the words *a light spanking*. She would run the gamut of resistance, refusal, curiosity, desire until, hopefully, desire would win out.

Sure enough, not five minutes passed before she said again, "A light spanking. Maybe I could do that." She looked around the club and then from one guy to the other. "Where would we do it?"

"Right here," Steve said, patting the couch.

"Right here?" she repeated. "In front of all these people?"

"No one's paying any attention to us, Shea," Zach said with a smile. "They're kind of busy, don't you think?" He waved toward the various scene stations where leather-clad and half-naked people were busy with rope, chain and impact toys, none of them even remotely interested in the three fully clothed people chatting on the observation couch.

"We could always go into a private scene room, if you're more comfortable with that," Steve added.

"No," Shea said quickly. She drew in a breath and blew it out, a resolute expression moving over her face. "Don't I need, um, like a safeword or something?"

Steve chuckled. "You're not going to need a safeword for a little spanking."

"But if that makes you more comfortable," Zach interjected, "then by all means, tell us your safeword."

"I don't have a," Shea began, but then amended, "I mean, my safeword is"—she paused a fraction of a second and then concluded—"zirconium."

Zach looked puzzled. "Zir-whaty-um?"

"Zirconium," Steve repeated. "It's a metal—a chemical element, right?"

"That's right," Shea said, flashing him a very pretty, dimpled smile. "Zr in the periodic table. I'm a scientist," she added.

Of course you are, Steve thought, mildly amused.

"Very cool," Zach said sincerely. "If you say your safeword, all action stops," he assured her. "That's a promise."

Shea bit her lip as she fought whatever internal battle was roiling inside her. Steve and Zach waited silently for her decision, as neither of them believed in pressuring a sub, especially a newbie. She had to offer herself freely, or not at all.

Finally Shea gave a small, determined nod. "Yes, okay," she said.

"Let's try the experiment."

Shea stood and smoothed the flowing skirt of her short dress over her thighs. Though she looked like a deer caught in the headlights, she slipped off her heels as Steve moved to the center of the couch and patted his thighs in invitation.

Zach rose from the couch and helped Shea drape herself over Steve's lap. She had a full, voluptuous figure, her ass ample and perfect for spanking. Though Steve normally favored more slender, narrow-hipped girls, he found himself quite attracted to Shea O'Connor, and his cock nudged appreciatively as she settled over him.

Zach crouched on the floor beside them and leaned close to Shea. "Steve will start easy and work up to more, based on how you're doing, okay?" He tucked an escaped tendril of hair behind her ear.

"Okay," Shea replied in a small voice.

Steve began to lift the hem of her dress with the intention of pulling down her panties, but Shea jerked up and twisted her head back in alarm, her hands flying to keep her ass covered. "No!" she cried. "Just over the dress. I'm not ready for more than that."

Steve lifted an eyebrow. He was about to explain that he always insisted on skin-on-skin contact, but Zach shot him a look and gave a small, quick shake of his head.

"All right," Steve acquiesced. "We can start that way."

He began lightly, really just patting her ass over the fabric of her dress with the flat of his palm while Zach stroked her back and shoulders. After a while, she relaxed against him, cradling her face in her arms. He increased the impact slowly until he finally brought down the first satisfying smack, which sent a pleasant jolt through his cock.

Shea stiffened and emitted a small gasp.

Zach stroked her back. "Shh, relax," he soothed.

Steve smacked her again, this time several good hard whacks.

"Oh! Oh, oh, oh!" Shea squeaked as she wriggled beneath his hand.

"That's it," Zach said calmly as he stroked her head. "You're doing great." He gave Steve a nod.

Steve was dying to pull up that stupid dress and yank down her panties, but he managed to control himself. He hit her hard through the layers of fabric, cupping his palm to increase the sting.

As he spanked the girl, he thought about how to reach her, to convince her of the need for skin-on-skin contact. Leaning over Shea, he said softly into her ear, "You would experience the sensation more authentically without the buffer of your skirt and panties, Shea. It would give you a better understanding of the process."

The girl didn't respond. She was breathing hard, her face hidden against her arms.

Taking this nonresponse as tacit permission, Steve lifted the hem of her dress. Shea didn't move. Beneath the dress, she wore a pair of pink cotton panties that fully covered her ample ass cheeks. Steve glanced at Zach, who was grinning.

What the fuck? Zach mouthed silently. Steve knew what Zach was thinking, because he was thinking the same thing: who over the age of twelve wore cotton briefs, especially to a BDSM sex club? Yet, Steve was both curiously touched by the simple panties and intensely turned on. Could this girl possibly be as innocent as she appeared? Would Zach and he be the first to introduce her to the undeniable power and passion of BDSM?

His balls tight with anticipation, Steve slipped his fingers beneath the elastic waistband of Shea's underwear.

All at once, she jerked her head up from her arms and twisted back, her entire body stiffening. "No!" she cried. "Not my panties. I didn't say my panties."

Steve removed his hand, forcing himself to resist the nearly overpowering impulse to ignore her. He pressed his lips together to keep from snapping at her.

"Sorry about that, Shea," Zach said, coming to the rescue. "We didn't mean to move too fast. Panties stay on. We got it."

"Okay, then," Shea said sulkily as she flashed a glare in Steve's direction.

He met her gaze calmly.

Turning away, Shea lowered her head once more into her arms.

If she were his, he would never tolerate such sass, but he reminded himself this was just a scene, a very casual scene with a total stranger. He would take it—and her—on its own terms.

Steve cupped his palm and let it crash against her left buttock, his cock shooting to attention as the impact forced her hard against his thighs, her round ass cheeks jiggling. He began again to smack her in a steady, hard rhythm as Zach spoke in a soft, soothing patter.

Shea was breathing hard, nearly panting. The backs of her thighs had turned a pretty shade of dark pink. Heat radiated from beneath her silly cotton underwear. Unable to resist another second, Steve again reached for the waistband of her panties, this time yanking them down before she could stop him to reveal an ass just as red as her thighs.

"Zirconium!" Shea cried as she reached back wildly to bat his hands away. In the next instant, she rolled abruptly from Steve's lap and onto Zach, who reached out in an effort to catch her.

Pulling away from him, she shot to her feet, her eyes wild, the flush on her cheeks, throat and chest giving her the mottled appearance of a post-orgasmic woman.

Zach, too, had risen quickly to his feet. He reached out to place steadying hands on the girl's shoulder. "Hey, calm down, Shea. Everything's okay. Really, it is. You need to take a deep breath."

Steve stood as well, furious at himself for pushing her too fast. "I apologize, Shea. I overstepped."

"No, it's okay," she said breathlessly, taking a step back so Zach's hands fell away. She slipped her feet into her shoes, reaching down with one hand to adjust one of them and nearly losing her balance in the process. "It's not you. It's just..." She trailed off as she reached for her purse. Hugging it to her chest, she continued, "I was wrong about this whole thing. It's too much. I can't— I just— I have to go."

Steve slipped his hand into his back pocket and pulled out one of their calling cards. "Here," he said, holding it out to her. "Take this. I hope you'll give us—and yourself—another chance. I sense something powerful in you, Shea—something we need to explore."

Without looking at it, Shea slipped the card into her clutch. "I have to go," she whispered again, both yearning and confusion in her eyes.

"It's okay. We understand," Zach said kindly. "Don't be a stranger."

With a last look at each of them, she slipped away.

Once she was gone, they both sank onto the sofa. Steve blew out a breath of frustration as Zach pushed his hair out of his eyes, not noticing that it immediately flopped back again.

"Jesus," Zach exclaimed. "What the hell just happened? She was doing great."

"She was afraid," Steve said.

"Of us?"

"Of herself," Steve replied.

~*~

"Oh my god, oh my god, oh my god, I can't believe I did that. I can't believe I did that."

Shea gripped the steering wheel of her parked car and banged her forehead lightly against it three times. She was still breathing too fast from having sprinted up the stairs of the club and out into the parking lot like a madwoman. Though the evening was cool, she was sweating, her heart still pounding. She needed some water. She needed cookies.

"No," she admonished herself aloud. "You've been so good. Don't fuck it up now."

I've just had my first spanking and I freaked out and ruined everything, she reminded herself. *Cookies are called for.*

Leaning across the gearshift, she reached for the emergency package of Oreos she kept in the glove compartment and tore open the cellophane. She grabbed two cookies and popped them, one after the other, into her mouth.

As she chewed the crunchy chocolate wafers and lovely cream filling, she began to relax a little. Before closing the bag, she took out six more cookies.

As she ate them, the usual guilt about eating junk food began to rear its ugly head, but she pushed it away. She needed those cookies after what she'd been through. She had earned them.

She picked up the bottle of water from its holder and took a drink. She became aware that her ass cheeks and thighs were stinging. She shifted on the leather and readjusted her short dress, a dress she had bought just for this occasion and would probably never wear again.

"Oh my god," she said again as the whole astonishing scene scrolled past her mind's eye. "I can't believe I did that."

Shea had fantasized for years about just such a scenario, and now that she had actually made it happen, she'd blown it.

Well, that wasn't exactly true. The scenario she'd imagined, the one she masturbated to at night before going to sleep, only involved one guy—a tall, dark and handsome guy who sometimes looked like Zac Ephron and sometimes like Cary Grant, depending on her mood. In her fantasy, he takes the champagne flute from her hand and sets it on the table. He pulls her into an embrace and kisses her until she loses her breath. Then he swoops her into his arms and carries her, effortlessly—she would weigh thirty pounds less than she actually did, of course—to the huge bed they share in their penthouse apartment in New York City or the Italian villa they go to in the winter. He makes her undress in front of him—a slow, sexy striptease—and then he orders her to lie across his lap.

He starts the spanking slowly, the same way Steve had, except he also lets his fingers slip between her legs. He alternates the pleasure and the pain, smacking her, then stroking her, until she's nearly crying with the need to come.

"Beg me," he whispers, and she does, and then she comes.

Real life always returned at that point, and she was still alone in her bed in her small Portland apartment.

Another fantasy was darker, and the man in that one had no face. He is there when she opened the door to her apartment, pulling her inside before she even had a chance to take the key from the lock.

He slams the door and pushes her hard against it. When she starts to protest, to scream, he slaps her across the face and then presses his hand hard over her mouth to muffle her cries. His other hand comes to her throat, and he catches her beneath the jaw so she can't breathe.

"I'm going to take my hand from your mouth," he says, his voice low, hard and sexy. "And you're not going to make a sound." He squeezes harder, her very life in his powerful hand. "Understand?"

She nods, barely able to move her head. He takes his hand from her throat, but only long enough to rip her clothes away. He forces her to the floor, holding her down with one hand while he pulls off his shirt and jeans. He rises over her, revealing his hard, muscular body and huge, erect cock. His hand once more on her throat, he slaps her thighs hard to make her open her legs, and then he forces himself inside her as he covers her mouth with his to stifle her terrified cries.

Shea's hand had slipped into her panties. She stroked her sopping wet pussy as the fantasy followed its much worn path in her mind.

A sudden rapping on her window caused Shea to yank her hand from beneath her dress with a cry. She whipped her head toward the sound.

Two young women were standing outside her car, concerned looks on their faces. Shea couldn't open the window without the car being on, and for a second, she just stared at them until her brain kicked back into action enough to allow her to open her door a crack.

"Is something wrong?" she asked, wondering if the heat in her face showed in the glare of the parking lot lights.

"Are you okay?" one of the girls asked. "We were just having a cigarette when we saw you run out of the club and to your car a few minutes ago."

"Then when you just sat in your car for so long, we were, like, you know, worried you were sick or something," the other girl said.

A flurry of thoughts and emotions rushed through Shea— embarrassment and annoyance at their intrusion on her privacy, appreciation that they'd noticed and cared about another woman who might be in distress, and disgusted anger that the two girls, who definitely should have known better, were smoking cigarettes. She tried to harness the better of her emotions as she replied, "Oh, no, I'm fine. Really. I just—I just needed some air, is all."

Grabbing her bag, she fumbled for her key and slid it into the ignition, praying the car would behave. The car started and she smiled at the girls. "Thanks, though, for looking out for me. That was really nice of you."

With a wave to the retreating girls, Shea pulled the door shut and put the car in reverse. As she drove out of the parking lot and onto the streets of Portland, her mind returned to Hardcore, and the two guys who had appeared out of nowhere and offered to scene with her.

To scene with her!

It sounded so sexy and sophisticated. She, Shea O'Connor, had been in a scene, a BDSM scene! People really did this stuff, and not just in fantasy.

Her thoughts segued to the couple at the whipping station. They'd been engaged in a lot more than just a little spanking. Jesus, the guy had used a bullwhip on that woman. He'd left marks—raised red welts that had to hurt like hell. And the woman had liked it. No, she had *loved* it.

Shea's pussy pulsed at the memory. As scary and astonishing as it had been to watch such an intense scene just a few yards away from her, it had also been exciting, even thrilling.

Zach Wilder and Steve Hartman. They were good names. Romance novel names. Master Zach and Sir Stephen. Sir Stephen, like in *Story of O*!

She would never want to be like O, though. O was stupid. O let herself be passed around like an object. She let René just hand her off to Sir Stephen—a guy who didn't care a thing about her, except as a total object. Not even a sex object—just an object to be used and discarded. Sir Stephen even had his maid whip her when he didn't feel like it. What kind of man did that?

But she'd loved the book, just the same. She couldn't lie—not anymore.

She was the new Shea O'Connor. The scientist who didn't shy away from her feelings, but instead explored them so she could better understand her own psyche and motivations.

She had lied for years, both to herself and the guys she occasionally went out with—though with them it was a lie of omission. She'd told herself her fantasies were sick and needed to be ignored. She'd told herself they were what was preventing her from finding a boyfriend, from finding love, but she was coming to understand at last, at her ripe old age of twenty-eight, that she was never going to find love if she didn't first understand herself.

She pulled into the parking lot at the back of her apartment building and slid into her assigned space in the carport. As she reached for her purse, she saw the small, white card on the passenger seat beside it. It must have fallen out when she was getting her keys. She picked it up and read it.

Steve Hartman/Zach Wilder

Professional BDSM training

Explore the passion and the power of erotic submission

The flip side of the card included a phone number and email address.

What were these guys—professional Doms? Masters for hire? What did that even mean?

Whatever it meant, Shea couldn't deny she was deeply intrigued.

Maybe she could sign up for training. The possibility both excited and terrified her. She thought about the BDSM training site she occasionally visited—okay, that she constantly visited—where sub girls worked with a trainer who made them do all kinds of thrilling, sexy, submissive things. Did she really have the nerve to do something like that?

She looked at the card again, recalling the two handsome guys she had run away from, like Cinderella escaping the ball. She had to admit, exploring the passion and power of erotic submission did sound pretty darn good. At least in theory.

It was all too much to think about. She needed to take a deep breath and decompress.

Clutching the card, Shea climbed out of the car and made her way into her first-floor, one-bedroom apartment. She dropped her purse, keys and the card on the kitchen counter and went directly to the freezer. Yanking open the door, she rummaged behind the peas and fat-free, sugar-free, flavor-free ice-cream-like substance until she found the emergency stash of Ben & Jerry's Chunky Monkey.

Just a few spoonfuls to calm her nerves.

She took the carton to the counter and grabbed a spoon. The first bite was always the best. She moaned with pleasure as the wonderful creamy explosion of banana with chunks of fudge and walnuts melted in her mouth. As she ate, she slipped off her shoes, glad to be rid of the toe-pinching high heels.

She continued to mull over the evening, going over every moment with a fine-tooth comb. True, at first she'd said only over the dress, but then, when he'd lifted the hem, she hadn't protested. She should have spoken up, instead of just hiding her head in her arms.

Steve hadn't done anything wrong. He had followed her cues, and yes, she *had* wanted to feel his hand on her ass. The skin-on-skin, as he'd called it. She'd wanted it more than anything she'd ever wanted in her life.

Dropping the spoon into the nearly empty carton, Shea reached back to touch her bottom. The skin still stung a little, though it was no longer hot to the touch. Her pussy gave a throb as she saw herself draped over Steve's lap, his hand making such intimate contact with her body. Around thirty, he was about five foot ten, with longish, wavy blond hair. He exuded a kind of tamped down sex appeal, something in the set of his somewhat cruel mouth and the intense focus of his dark blue eyes. He'd looked good in his black leather pants and button-down black shirt, his forearms muscular and ropy with veins.

Zach appeared younger, somewhere in his midtwenties, she guessed. He was tall, maybe six foot four, with the build of a football player—massive shoulders and chest, narrow hips, muscular legs. He was more boyishly handsome than Steve, with an engaging smile and dark hair that hung down over his eyes. He had a beard—not the big, bushy beard some guys were wearing these days, but more of a two-week cover of sexy stubble that gave him a rakish appeal.

Her eye fell on the calling card Steve had given her as his parting words returned to her. *I hope you'll give us—and yourself—another chance. I sense something powerful in you, Shea—something we need to explore.*

He was right. She had come this far. She had embraced her deep-seated erotic urges and thrown herself headlong into researching the topic. She had learned she wasn't sick and twisted after all. She had discovered there were thousands—no, millions—who shared her needs and desires. She had found the courage to go into the field like an intrepid explorer. She had met two hot guys who were interested in scening with her. She had allowed them to spank her!

And yes, she had loved it, even while she'd been afraid.

What must they have thought of her when she cut things off so abruptly and fled the scene? Were they laughing about it now—about the newbie wannabe sub girl who ran away in the middle of a spanking?

What would they think if they knew she was still a virgin?

Chapter 2

That Monday morning, Shea stared at the vial containing the new chemical compound she'd been working on, wondering if she'd finally gotten it right after several days of trial and error. Her concentration had been off since she'd arrived at the lab, her mind constantly sliding back to Saturday night at Hardcore. The business card Steve had handed her was burning a hole in her purse. She'd handled it a dozen times and had almost made contact, but each time she'd chickened out at the last minute.

A heavy hand on her shoulder startled her, nearly making her drop the vial.

"We've got a problem, O'Connor," Scott Carroll, her boss at Cosmetic Formulations, boomed in his overloud voice. "Or rather, *you've* got a problem."

Jeff Scharnott, who sat one workstation over in the large lab, sniggered softly, no doubt pleased Shea, and not he, had been singled out for that morning's berating.

"What's that, Mr. Carroll?" Shea strove to keep her voice even and calm as she willed herself not to flush. Her boss sensed weakness like a hawk sighting its prey, and always pounced. "If it's the dimethicone adjustment, I'm aware of it and I think I'm almost there." She held up her vial as proof. "I'm satisfied the occlusive agents are properly balanced now with a good humectant."

Shea had helped in the development of several successful moisturizers for the company, but this was the first time she'd been entrusted with such a complicated formulation. When she'd been given the assignment for the latest product commissioned by a top cosmetic company, she'd been both thrilled and terrified. The lotion was supposed to be a toner, serum and moisturizer in one, formulated to hydrate combination and oily skin while toning, reducing breakouts, treating sun damage and calming irritated skin. Oh, and it needed to smell good, too.

"We've got deadlines, O'Connor. The test groups are being lined up as we speak. Your scent is too floral. Fix it. The client wants a clean, fresh scent, something in the cucumber family with maybe a trace of citrus. If you need to pull an all-nighter—do it. Just don't expect any overtime."

"I'm on it, Mr. Carroll," Shea said, willing him to walk away. She loved her job, but her boss was another story. She hated the way he called everyone by their last names, and seemed unable to modulate his voice, booming like a drill sergeant so that everyone in the lab heard every word he said. He was always quick to criticize and his rare compliments were usually backhanded and left you unsure if you'd just been praised or humiliated.

He grunted and turned his attention to Jeff. "Hey, Scharnott, you working hard or hardly working?"

Relieved she was no longer the focus of attention, Shea returned to her task, but her mind continued to drift back to the night at the club, and the two men who had taken such sexy control over her. She knew what she needed to do to get back on track with her work. She would just take care of it, and then she would be able to concentrate.

She waited until the boss had left the lab, grabbed her purse and slid from the tall stool at her workstation.

As she passed Jeff's station, he said, "You going to the break room? Bring me back a cup of coffee. You know how I like it—cream and three sugars."

Jeff was always telling Shea to get him something or handle some trivial formulation for him, as if she were his personal lab assistant. When she had first joined the staff two years before, fresh from graduate school, she had made the mistake of obliging him. Now, without breaking her stride, she said, "Sorry, I'm busy. Get your own coffee."

Shea headed for the women's restroom. One advantage of being the only woman in her lab was that she generally had the bathroom all to herself. She entered a stall and closed and locked the door. Setting her purse on the floor, she removed her lab coat and hung it on the door hook.

Reaching for her purse, she rummaged at the bottom of the large bag for the plastic cosmetic case that held her favorite travel toy—her trusty purple plastic pussy teaser. It was a G-spot vibrator with a slim, seven-inch shaft and a one-and-a-half inch egg-shaped head. She removed the toy, along with the small tube of lubricant.

Closing the toilet lid, she lifted her skirt and pulled down her panties. Standing in front of the toilet, she put one foot up on the seat and carefully inserted the vibrator into her already-wet pussy. Sitting carefully, she perched on the edge of the seat. Reaching between her spread legs, she twisted the base of the dildo to turn it on, sighing with pleasure as it began to vibrate inside her.

As she rubbed her clit, she let the new fantasy that had been fueled by the events of Saturday night scroll through her mind like an X-rated movie in which she had the starring role.

Naked, she's hanging from chains by her cuffed wrists, spread eagle, her feet barely touching the ground. Her slender, perfect body is bathed in sweat and stippled with welts. Each crack of the bullwhip yanks a cry from her lips, but her pussy is swollen and throbbing, its juices wetting the insides of her thighs.

Sir Stephen is relentless, striking her again and again. Her heart is pounding as the whip cuts into her flesh. She's trembling in her bonds, sweat stinging her eyes and plastering her hair to her forehead, but she won't use her safeword, no way. Not this time.

Master Zach appears in front of her and takes her face in his hands. He dips his head and brings his mouth to her lips. Their kiss is long and passionate, and Shea forgets the pain of the whip, or rather, the pain melds into the pleasure of her lover's kiss.

The whip, the kiss, the throb of her clit, Master Zach's tender touch, Sir Stephen's relentless stroke...

"Oh god," Shea whispered as the pussy teaser vibrated inside her. "Oh, yesssss." The orgasm was powerful, if brief, and she shuddered as it washed over and through her.

She turned off the vibrator with trembling fingers and slid it out of her still-thrumming pussy. Standing, she pulled up her panties and smoothed down her skirt. Leaving her coat and purse in the stall for the moment, she moved toward the bank of sinks. She turned on the hot water in one of the sinks and squeezed a large dollop of liquid soap over the plastic dildo.

As she washed her toy, she regarded herself in the mirror. Her cheeks and neck were mottled with telltale color. Not for the first time, she wondered about formulating a foundation that would effectively hide flushed skin without making you look like a cadaver. Would there be a market for such a product? Well, definitely a market of at least one.

Once she was satisfied the vibrator was properly cleaned, she dried it with paper towels and returned to the stall. She placed it and the tube of lubricant in their case and pushed the case down into the bottom of her bag. As she started to zip the purse closed, her gaze fell on the much-handled calling card.

She plucked the card from her bag and stared at it for the hundredth time.

Steven Hartman/Zach Wilder

Professional BDSM training

Explore the passion and the power of erotic submission

She flipped the card over, though she'd already memorized the phone number and email address.

"Just do it," she said aloud. "You know you want to."

Suddenly resolved, she grabbed her phone from her lab coat pocket and opened the messaging app. Before she could talk herself out of it yet again, she texted rapidly with her thumbs.

"Hi. This is Shea from the other night at Hardcore. Remember me?"

~*~

Steve was in the middle of grinding a spring steel reinforced cane handle when his cell phone buzzed in his pocket. He ignored it at first, intent on finishing his task.

Zach sat across from him at the long table in the Leather Master's workshop, busy measuring and cutting a kangaroo hide from Australia. Taggart, the Leather Master, was at the other end of the workshop, putting the finishing touches on a hanging row of eight-plaited snake whips.

The phone buzzed again. Removing his work gloves, Steve reached into his jeans pocket and pulled it out. The screen indicated he had a text message from a number he didn't recognize. He opened the app and read the short message, his eyes widening with pleasure and surprise.

"Well, will you look at this," he said, holding the phone out toward Zach. "I wasn't sure we'd hear from her again."

Zach lifted his head from his work and squinted as he read the words on the screen. His lips lifted into a smile. "Sweet," he said. "So, text her back. See if she wants to come over."

Though they both now worked full time in Taggart's whip making business, they continued to engage in their semi-professional pastime of training both men and women in the local BDSM community who wanted to learn about or expand their understanding of erotic Domination and submission. They made contacts at Hardcore, the Portland Power Exchange events and at the whip demos they now regularly participated in for the Leather Master's business.

It was a great way to stay connected to the community, as well as indulge in their sadistic and dominant predilections. They were careful to keep sex out of the equation, at least during the training process, both keenly aware of their responsibility as Doms not to take advantage of the particular vulnerability of a submissive in training.

For Zach, it had been a great way to hook up with potential play partners after the training was over, since the women had already been thoroughly vetted by the pair. Until fairly recently, that perk hadn't been something Steve had cared about, since he'd been in a serious relationship with the submissive woman he'd thought he would eventually marry.

That was, until he'd read an email she'd left open on his laptop. Unbeknownst to Steve, Sandra had an online lover she'd apparently been having a torrid virtual affair with for several months. She had already made plans to secretly meet "Evil Master," as the asshole styled himself, in person on her next business trip to the East Coast.

She claimed she'd left the email open by accident, never properly explaining why she had used his computer instead of her own. Accident or no, the consequences had been devastating, their relationship effectively over. Sandra had tearfully said she'd cancel her plans to meet Evil Master, but Steve had told her to go ahead.

In retrospect, there had been signs of Sandra's discontent and secret betrayal before she'd thrust it right under his nose, but that hadn't made it hurt any less. He had been devastated at the time, but had been slowly coming to realize it was more about his ego than his heart.

"What've we got going tonight?" Steve asked, since Zach always had a better handle on that than he did. "Do we have any clients?"

Zach picked up his cell phone from the worktable and tapped at the screen. He shook his head. "Nothing on the schedule tonight. How about we grab a bite or a drink after work—keep it low key and see where we go from there?"

Steve nodded. "Good idea. We'll take it slower this time, now that we know she's skittish." He typed back a quick text.

"Hi, Shea. This is Steve. Zach and I were just talking about you. We'd love to meet you for dinner or a drink or something, maybe after work today? Are you free?"

The little dots began to undulate immediately, indicating she was texting back. *"I might have to work a little late tonight, but I should be free by eight. We could meet at Grassa over on Washington Street. Do you know it?"*

"Sure. That sounds perfect. Shall we say 8:30?"

"Sounds good. See you both then."

~*~

The guys were already at the restaurant when Shea finally arrived at eight forty. They were seated at a table near the bar, and Zach lifted his hand in greeting as she approached. They both stood when she got to the table, and Steve actually pulled out her chair for her. Shea, used to the socially awkward science geeks that surrounded her at work, was both startled and charmed by their old-fashioned politeness.

"I'm so sorry I'm late," she said as she sat down. "Work was crazy." In fact, she could have been there on time, even early, but she'd raced back to her apartment instead. No way was she going to show up wearing her boring work clothes.

She'd changed into a blue, sleeveless silk top that always garnered compliments, worn untucked over a flowing black skirt. The skirt was a tiny bit snug at the waist but the top was loose enough to hide the muffin-top effect. She'd even changed into the sexy panties and bra set she should have worn to the club—not because she planned to flash them at the restaurant, but because they made her feel more confident and attractive.

"No problem," Zach said with a smile. Now that she could see him better in the light of the restaurant rather than the dim, reddish haze of the club, she saw he was older than she'd initially thought, probably closer to thirty than twenty-five, but still just as good-looking with his mop of dark hair flopping into his eyes, his closely cropped beard, , dancing eyes and big bear of a body it would be nice to snuggle against.

"This is a great place you selected," Steve said, drawing her attention to him. He was good-looking, too, she decided, though in a different way, with his narrow features, chiseled edges and a lean, hard body. Both guys had mugs of beer in front of them. Following her gaze, Steve added, "Fantastic selection of local craft beers here. Hope you don't mind we started without you." He lifted his half-empty mug.

"No problem," Shea assured him. "I'm glad you did. Did you order dinner yet?"

"Waiting for you," Steve replied. He glanced around and caught the eye of a waitress, who came over to the table.

Shea considered getting a beer to calm her nerves, but reminded herself she had to drive, and instead ordered an iced tea. For dinner, Zach chose the pork belly mac and cheese, Steve got the mushroom cannelloni and Shea ordered the grilled chicken piccata.

"So," Zach said, once the waitress had set a glass of tea in front of Shea and brought another beer for each of the guys, "what is it you do that keeps you at work so late?"

"I'm a chemist," Shea said. "I work for a cosmetic lab."

"Wow, sounds fancy," Zach said. "You must be smart."

Shea shrugged. "I've always been good with numbers and science, but really, I just like to mix things up and see what happens."

"Please tell me you don't test mascara on bunny rabbits," Steve said with a teasing grin.

Still, Shea took the question seriously. "No," she said emphatically. "Zero animal testing at my company. That's one reason I took the job."

"So you try out the mascara on yourself," he amended with a grin.

"Actually, I specialize in emulsions and surfactants," Shea said.

Steve nodded but Zach looked puzzled.

"Soaps, moisturizers, lip balms—stuff like that," she clarified. "I'm working on a big project right now for a top manufacturer. It's pretty exciting." She almost started to expand on the topic, but brought herself up short. These guys didn't want to hear about skin creams. Seeking a quick change of topic, she said, "And what about you two? That card was intriguing." Lowering her voice, she continued, "Are you, like, professional BDSM trainers? Is that even legal?"

"We don't charge for the training," Steve explained.

"It's purely a labor of love," Zach added with a smile.

"Though we do occasionally rent out the BDSM dungeon we have in our basement," Steve continued.

"*Our* basement?" Shea echoed. "What are you guys, brothers or something?" *Or gay? Oh, shit. Are they gay? Did I somehow miss the cues? Wait a minute, it's okay if they're gay. It's not like you're going to have a relationship with either one of them.*

Both guys smiled. "No," Zach replied. "We're not brothers, and no, we're not gay."

Shea felt herself coloring. Was she that obvious? She picked up her iced tea, lifting it to her lips to hide her face.

"Actually, we connected because of our work. We both make whips and other impact toys and BDSM gear. We met at a trade show a few years back and hit it off. Steve bought this great house over in Healy Heights a few years ago and the lease on my place was up. We already got along really great by then. Steve had the space and didn't mind having a roommate"—Zach shrugged—"and so I moved in. The BDSM dungeon came afterward and things just sort of evolved from there."

Steve nodded. "To answer your question more completely, we do work with people who are interested in learning more about both sides of the D/s equation, but we don't charge for our services. We've both been active in the scene for a long time, and there are a lot of folks out there who are interested, but kind of clueless."

"Like me," Shea interjected with a self-effacing grin.

Steve neither agreed with nor denied her assertion. "We've found that just because you're interested in BDSM, that doesn't mean you suddenly know how to be a good sub or, for that matter, a good Dom. In some ways, being a good Dom is more important, because they have the ultimate responsibility in the relationship to keep things safe, sane and consensual."

"That makes sense," Shea said, intrigued. "So, what, you have classes and stuff? Dominance 101? Submission for Dummies?"

Zach laughed and took up the thread. "Something like that. Except we find it's most effective to work one-on-one with someone, rather than in a class scenario. Though we do work with couples sometimes."

"We'd love to work with you, Shea," Steve added. "I'm sorry things turned out as they did the other night, but I hope you'll give us another chance. I wasn't lying when I said I sensed something powerful in you, something we should explore further. If I had to guess, I'd say, in spite of your lack of direct experience, you're a natural submissive." He regarded her intently.

Shea stared back, unable to look away. "Natural submissive," she whispered, the words reverberating in her soul.

"Yes," Steve said softly. "Since you were sexually aware, you have dreamed of kneeling in front of a strong, dominant man, a man who understood your deep-seated need to give of yourself, to lay yourself bare to his touch, his lash, his every command."

"Oooh," Shea whispered, the word pulled from somewhere deep inside her. Her nipples ached suddenly, her clit throbbing gently in her sexy new silk panties.

The waitress appeared, startling Shea as she set her meal before her. She asked them if they needed anything else and poured more iced tea into Shea's glass before drifting away.

The mood was broken, which was both a disappointment and a relief, but left Shea longing for more.

Both guys tucked at once into their food, and she picked up her knife and fork. The chicken was delicious, but though she'd been starving a moment before, now Shea didn't have much of an appetite.

She cast several sidelong glances at the guys as they ate, hardly able to believe she was actually sitting there with two authentic BDSM trainers. What had always been a fantasy, a daydream, was now being dangled in front of her, no apparent strings attached.

Or were there?

"Um, about this training thing," she finally said. Both men looked up at her, waiting for her to continue. "How does it work exactly? Do I just show up at your dungeon for a session or something?" She thought about the research she had done online regarding the scene. "What about my limits and boundaries? Is this just training or do you expect, uh, sexual favors?"

Even as these stupid words tumbled out of her mouth, the familiar, unwelcome heat of a blush moved over her cheeks and throat. *Sexual favors?* Who used words like that? They were going to think she was such an idiot.

Zach put down his fork and regarded her seriously. "These are all excellent questions," he said, and though Shea searched his face to see if he was making fun of her, all she saw was kindness. "The way it works is we would conduct an initial interview to figure out where you are in all this. We would talk about your past experience and what you hope to get out of the training. Because of the nature of the relationship, it's essential that you're open and honest with us about what you're seeking and, as you mentioned, what your boundaries and limits are."

"As to sex," Steve added, "that depends how you define sex. If you mean do we expect you to pay us in either money or, uh, sexual favors"—his mouth quirked into a half smile as he repeated her ridiculous words—"absolutely not. We do this because we love BDSM and we've found there's a need in the community for the kind of services we offer. That said, you *will* be expected to submit and obey during the training process. And, make no mistake, BDSM is by its very nature a sexually charged activity. That means, within the boundaries and limits we all agree to, you will be expected to be naked in front of us. You will allow us to touch you as is appropriate in the course of training. Depending how far we go with this, a part of submission includes explicit sexual training, but that's something we could negotiate in the future."

"In other words," Zach continued, "yes, BDSM training is sexual but no, we will not expect you to have sex with us as a part of the process."

Shea looked down at her nearly untouched food as she thought about it. It was kind of weird that they worked together. Did it really take two Doms to train a sub? By the same token, she took comfort from the fact she wouldn't be alone with either one of them. It was less likely that things would get complicated.

In fact, she was being offered an ideal scenario—real submissive training, just like that cool slave training site she'd found on the Internet—without the drama and messiness of an actual relationship.

Zach was the first to break the silence. "So what do you think? Are you interested in coming by our dungeon to see what it's all about?"

Shea looked up. They were both staring at her as if they could see past the bones of her face directly into her mind. As she stared back, her heart began to hammer.

In every other aspect of her life, when she wanted something, she had gone for it with everything she had. She'd held herself back far too long in this one area and now she was being offered the chance of a lifetime. Admittedly, she barely knew these two guys, but her gut told her she could trust them.

Shea screwed up her courage, blew out a breath and said, "Yes, I'm interested. Very interested."

"Great," both guys said in unison, which made her laugh in spite of her nerves.

Zach pulled out his cell phone and tapped at the screen. "We're free most nights this week." He looked up at her. "What about you?"

Aware she might lose her courage if she waited another minute, much less another day, Shea blurted, "How about now?"

"Now works," Steve said.

He waved at the waitress, who made her way toward them.

"You want that to go, honey?" she asked, pointing to Shea's plate.

"You hardly ate," Zach commented. "Didn't you like it?"

"No, it was delicious," Shea said. "I, uh, I just wasn't as hungry as I thought." To the waitress, she said, "Sure, that would be good, thanks." She could have it for lunch tomorrow.

When the waitress returned with Shea's doggy bag and the check, neither guy would let her pay, which, again, surprised and charmed her.

"We live about fifteen minutes from here," Zach said as they left the restaurant together. "I could go with you in your car, if you want."

"No, that's okay," Shea said quickly, thinking about the empty soda cans and candy wrappers on her passenger seat. "I'll just follow you guys."

As they drove in tandem along the streets of Portland, Shea kept up a running conversation with herself. "I can't believe you're doing this." She repeated this aloud several times in a row before finally replying, "Why can't you believe it? *I* can't believe you waited until you were practically thirty to finally act on your fantasies."

She shivered as Steve's words echoed in her head. *A natural submissive... Since you were sexually aware, you have dreamed of kneeling in front of a strong, dominant man, a man who understood your deep-seated need to give of yourself, to lay yourself bare to his touch, his lash, his every command.*

"But what if I can't do it?" she asked herself in the rearview mirror. "I freaked out over a little spanking."

But that wasn't true. It wasn't the spanking that had freaked her out. The spanking had been wonderful—even more thrilling than her wildest fantasies.

What had freaked her out was the thought of the two of them seeing her naked butt. She had been too vulnerable, too nervous, to let that happen, even though she understood intellectually that it was no big deal. Everyone was naked all the time in the scene, at least so it seemed to her.

Tonight was just the interview, they'd said, but who knew what a trainee interview entailed? Would she be expected to strip? What if she lost her nerve? She should've had that beer or glass of wine. Courage in a bottle.

But, no. She knew herself better than that. Alcohol didn't make her braver. It just made her stupid. Better to have full control of her faculties. She was a grown woman. These guys were professionals. They weren't expecting perfection from her. They knew what they were getting into. If they didn't like what they saw, too bad for them.

Gripping this false bravado like a lifeline, Shea pulled into the driveway of a two-story stone house in a much nicer neighborhood than she lived in, though even her neck of the woods was being gentrified, which meant her rent would increase yet again when her lease was up in a few months.

The guys parked in the garage beside a second car and gestured for her to come into the house that way. "The stairs to the dungeon are just off the kitchen," Zach explained as they led her inside.

The kitchen was small but clearly had been updated, with granite counters, dark wood cabinets and a large gas range. "You want some wine or something?" Steve asked as he hung the keys to the car on a hook just inside the door.

Again, Shea was tempted, but said, "No, thanks. I'm good."

"Okay. We have bottled water downstairs."

Shea followed them down a set of wooden stairs into a room with concrete floors and walls, a large washer and dryer against one wall, a counter with a built-in sink on an adjacent wall, and an ancient oil-burning boiler off to the side.

"The dungeon is this way," Zach said, heading toward a set of double doors at the back of the room.

With Zach in front of her and Steve behind, Shea entered the room, eyes wide with anticipation. The space was set up much as it had been at Hardcore, with scene stations containing various BDSM furniture.

While Shea's scientific mind noted and categorized the inventory—a St. Andrew's cross, a spanking bench, a suspension rack, a bondage table, a standing cage just big enough to hold one person—her emotions took off in their own direction. A powerful electric current of delight, fear, anticipation, longing and awe arced wildly through her. It was as if the lights had been switched on after a lifetime in the dark.

"Come over here," Zach said. They led her to a couch set against the back wall. When Shea started to take a seat, Steve stopped her, gripping her upper arm gently but firmly.

"Subs don't sit on the furniture in this room, Shea." His voice was different suddenly—deeper and more assured. Something in Shea thrilled to the sound, though at the same time her heart began to hammer in her chest.

He pointed to a black mat in front of the couch. "Remove your shoes and stand on the kneeling pad, arms clasped loosely behind your back while we conduct the interview. We'll ask you some questions and give you a few simple exercises to get a better sense of where you are and what you need."

Steve released her arm and took a seat on the couch. Zach sat down beside him. Both of them stared up at her. Steve cocked an eyebrow. "Shea? Is there a problem?"

She looked from one guy to another as she willed herself to obey. *You can do this,* she urged herself. *Don't fuck it up. Not this time.*

Her heart was now beating so loudly she was sure they could both hear it. Somehow, she managed to slip her sandals off her feet. She took a step, and then another, until she was standing on the mat. She put her hands behind her back and gripped them tightly together to stop the trembling. Lifting her chin, she prayed her voice wouldn't crack.

"No, Sir. There's no problem."

CHAPTER 3

Zach's balls tightened with anticipation as he regarded the woman standing before them. He loved the way her emotions played so openly over her face. She reminded him of a kid waiting in line to ride the largest roller coaster at the amusement park—terror and thrilled anticipation whirling through her as she inched closer and closer to the front of the line.

As his eyes moved over her full, heavy breasts and shapely hips, his thoughts shifted to the first time he'd been introduced to BDSM. A freshman in college, he'd been flattered by the attentions of the twenty-two-year-old grad student who had also attended the raucous frat party of an acquaintance whose name Zach no longer remembered.

He could still recall her voice—throaty and deep, filled with self-assurance. "Hey there, you. Football player." When he turned toward her with a *who me?* expression, she had nodded, her mouth lifting into a half smile. "Yeah, you. Get over here."

Being eighteen and thrilled by the attention of an attractive older woman, Zach had instantly approached her. Her greeting had been to reach up and wrap both hands around his neck to pull him down for a long, lingering kiss that included plenty of tongue. It was all the greeting he'd needed, and he'd followed her like a puppy dog as she led him to an empty bedroom on one of the upper floors of the sprawling old house.

She had pushed him inside and locked the door. Leaning against it, she'd announced, "I am Mistress Claire. I like to use boys for my pleasure. But first, they have to earn it. Are you prepared to earn your way into my bed?"

With no real idea what she was talking about, Zach had readily agreed to whatever she'd required, as long as it meant he got to fuck her. When she'd told him to strip and lie over her knees for a good old-fashioned spanking, he'd been both amused and intrigued. Whatever game she was playing, it was all right with him.

She had remained fully clothed in a short denim skirt and a silky black top as he had draped himself, naked and already sporting a full erection, over her thighs.

Though the spanking was mild enough, especially in retrospect, he had enjoyed its stinging heat and the sound of her hand striking his flesh. But even then he had known something was missing or rather something wasn't quite right with the setup.

Thoroughly aroused and operating primarily on instinct, he had rolled away from Claire and, before she realized what was happening, he had flipped her over his knees. He had yanked up her little skirt, delighted to discover she was wearing nothing beneath it.

Much bigger and stronger than she, he'd easily held her down with one hand as he'd spanked her, quite hard, with the other. At first she had yelped and cursed, but it wasn't long before she began to moan, her body gyrating beneath his palm as she ground her bare cunt against his leg. The sex afterward was explosive. It was, as Bogie might have said in an old movie, the beginning of a beautiful friendship.

They began to see each other regularly, though not exclusively. Mistress Claire continued to dom other guys, but with him, she was definitely a submissive. The relationship fizzled out after a few months, but by then Zach was firmly on his way to becoming a full-fledged Dom.

It was hard to believe eleven years had elapsed since that life-altering experience with Mistress Claire. He'd had plenty of sub girls since, sharing most of them with Steve in the past three years since they had become friends and training partners.

Zach was pleased that Steve was ready to get back into the game with Shea O'Connor, the pretty, voluptuous redhead who stood in front of them, shifting on her feet like a little kid waiting anxiously in the principal's office.

"You look a little nervous, Shea," Zach said. "I want you to take a few deep breaths and try to relax, okay? This is just a getting-to-know-you session—no pressure."

Shea flashed him a grateful glance. She drew in a deep breath and let it out slowly, pursing her lips as she exhaled.

"Again," Zach encouraged. "Deep breaths. In... And out. That's it."

When she appeared to have calmed a little, he said, "First, some very basic questions—are you single?"

"Yes."

"How old are you?"

"Twenty-eight."

He had assumed she was younger based on her apparent innocence and lack of experience. Keeping his surprise off his face, he continued, "We want to get a better sense of where you are in your submissive journey. Tell us more about your experience in the scene, other than Saturday night, I mean."

"I don't have any," she replied, looking down at her toes.

Whoa. That was a first in their training career. Most of the women they encountered in the scene had been involved in BDSM for a number of years and were looking for specific training in a particular area, such as caning, slave positions or sexual worship. Keeping his face neutral, Zach said, "That must have taken a lot of courage then, to submit to us as you did. I know things ended a little abruptly but—"

"I know," Shea blurted, cutting him off. "I'm so sorry I—"

"No apologies necessary," Zach interrupted. "A few ground rules I should have covered right off the bat. First off, during this interview, and in fact whenever you're in our dungeon, we do expect you to answer all questions honestly and thoroughly, but you will never interrupt or speak out of turn."

"Sorry," Shea mumbled, hunching her shoulders forward.

"Stand up straight, please," Steve interjected. "Shoulders back, chin raised. You are presenting yourself to your trainers."

They both waited as she straightened her posture. Color was seeping over her fair cheeks like spilled red ink.

Hoping to put her more at ease, Zach assured her, "What happened at the club was entirely our fault. It's hard sometimes, especially in a club atmosphere with so many distractions around us. We moved too fast."

"The rat's never wrong," Steve interjected.

Zach looked at him in confusion. "What the heck does that mean?"

Some of the anxiety had gone out of Shea's expression, replaced by sudden eagerness. "Excuse me," she said. "If I may…"

"By all means," Zach said, waiting to be enlightened.

"Steve's talking about the scientific method employed with lab rats. Right, Steve?" As Steve nodded, Shea continued, clearly now in her comfort zone, "It's all about project design, hypothesis and outcome. If you design a maze that the rat can't complete, it's not the rat's fault. Something is wrong with your design and execution."

Zach, who had attended college on a football scholarship and majored in physical education and partying, thought he understood what Shea was saying, but didn't want her to get too far off track. If she minded being the "rat" in this particular scenario, she didn't indicate it.

"Okay," he said with a shrug. "So, getting back to our topic, you've had no formal experience in the scene, but what about something more casual, you know, like maybe a past boyfriend liked to tie your wrists to the headboard or something? Or maybe you engaged in a little role-playing?"

Shea shook her head decisively. "No, nothing like that. Never. I guess my involvement to this point is more academic. I did some research online and I've read some books."

"But it goes deeper than that, surely, or you wouldn't be here," Steve said.

"Yes," Shea whispered.

Now they were getting somewhere. "Say you're masturbating," Zach said. "Tell us about your favorite sexual fantasies—the ones that make you come the hardest?"

The earlier blush had faded, but now returned with a vengeance. The girl would have made a terrible poker player. "My sexual fantasies when I masturbate?" she squeaked.

"Yes. That's what I said. It's okay, Shea. You're among friends here. You can trust us, I promise. We just want—we *need* to understand what makes you tick, you see? What moves you, what excites you, what frightens you. It's important underlying information to help us tailor a training package for you. All we want from you is honesty. There is no set script or right answer. Don't try to censor yourself or make it sound pretty. Just tell us the real, dark, gut-honest truth. What gets you going, Shea? What makes you come?"

She related an almost vanilla scenario of a fantastically handsome guy ordering her to strip in front of him so he could give her a slow, sensual spanking. Zach, who knew women, especially submissive women, doubted such a tame fantasy was all it took to get Shea off.

Steve, apparently on the same page, interrupted Shea as she was getting to the happily-ever-after part. "That's fine," he said. "Now tell us the real fantasy. The dark, dirty, gritty story that roars through your head like a freight train when you're alone at night in the dark, with no one around to judge or criticize. What is it that makes your heart pound and your cunt pulse?"

Shea's right hand appeared from behind her back and fluttered up to cover her mouth.

"Back in position," Steve snapped.

Shea obeyed, dropping her hand and reaching once more behind her back.

"Come on, Shea," Zach encouraged. "You know he's right. If you want to get anything out of this training, rigorous honesty is absolutely essential. Remember, we don't judge you. We're the same as you. We have the same buttons, just in reverse."

"Okay," she said at last. "Okay. I'll tell you." She drew in a deep breath and blew it out slowly. Looking down at the ground, she began to speak, her voice so low Steve and Zach both leaned forward to hear her better.

"I get home from work, and when I open the door, there's this stranger inside my apartment. It's dark and I can't see his face. He slams me against the wall, and when I start to scream, he slaps me across the face and then clamps his hand hard over my mouth. He brings his other hand up to my throat and he grips hard, so hard that I can't even take a breath. I'm terrified and my heart is pounding out of my chest.

"'I'm going to take my hand away from your mouth.' he says. 'You better not make a sound.' I nod"—she looks up at them—"I mean, what else can I do? He's big and strong and in control."

"Go on," Zach urged softly, his cock responding to her words.

"He throws me down to the floor and rips off all my clothes," Shea continued. "While I lie there naked and terrified, he pulls off his shirt and jeans. He's got big muscles and his cock is huge." Shea began to blush again, but her eyes were bright, her nipples poking against her silky top.

Ducking her head, she continued, "Sometimes he makes me suck his cock. He straddles my chest and rams his shaft down my throat, gagging me with it. Or sometimes he just forces himself between my legs and he-he—" She was suddenly breathless, apparently unable to continue. She looked up at them again, her expression beseeching.

"He claims you," Steve supplied in what Zach thought of as his calm sadist's voice. "Without mercy or concern for your pleasure."

"Yes," Shea breathed, her eyes shining. "Yes."

"Take off your clothing, Shea," Steve said, still in calm sadist mode. "Start with your top, and then your bra."

"What?" Shea squeaked.

"You didn't hear me?"

She didn't answer. She had come out of position again, her arms now wrapped around her torso.

"Come on, Shea," Zach soothed. "Surely you understood you would be asked to take off your clothes?"

"Yes, I know. But, if it's okay, I'd rather take off my skirt first."

Zach shook his head. If he'd misread her, and she was just a wannabe, it was better to find out now. "No, Shea. In this dungeon, you will obey our commands. You don't negotiate. Do as Steve says. Now."

Shea swallowed visibly, a war of emotions moving over her face. Tears actually sprang to her eyes and Zach felt sorry for her, though he didn't understand what exactly was wrong.

Finally, slowly, she reached for the hem of her top with trembling fingers.

~*~

Shea silently cursed both herself and the two men staring up at her with those complacent, smug expressions. Why had she worn this stupid skirt? It made her look fat. No—strike that—she *was* fat. She was a roly-poly fat piglet and now they were going to see the truth and then they would send her away.

If only she could have taken off the skirt first so there would be no bunching at the waist. Then she would have removed her bra, executing that particularly feminine maneuver of unhooking and pulling the bra through an armhole. If she had been the one in control, she could have distracted them.

Even as these tortured thoughts skittered through her mind on little rats' feet, she knew they were ridiculous. These guys were pros. Many of the women she'd seen at the BDSM club had been overweight, even more than she was. None of them had appeared the slightest bit self-conscious, dressed in tight-fitting leather or nothing at all.

Grabbing onto the strength of those women, Shea hauled herself back to a more rational place. It was exciting, even thrilling to be in a BDSM dungeon. She was no longer simply reading about it in books or watching it on the Internet or fantasizing about it alone in her bed.

She was with two bona fide Doms, both of whom were actually interested in training her. Instead of worrying about superficial things like her appearance, she would focus on behaving with as much poise as she could muster, even if it was just an act.

Shea pulled her top over her torso and head, sucking in her stomach as much as she could in the process. She couldn't quite meet the eyes of the two men watching her, but she could feel the burn of their intense gazes.

She dropped the shirt to the floor and reached back to unclasp the pretty pink lace bra she had worn "just in case." At least she looked good in that.

"Sweet," Zach said, drawing out the word with apparently sincere appreciation as Shea's large breasts bounced free of their confines.

"Beautiful," breathed Steve. "You have lovely breasts, Shea."

In spite of her nervousness, Shea smiled, warmth moving through her at their reactions.

"Now the skirt," said Zach. "And your panties."

Shea's mouth was dry. She licked her lips, her eyes flickering over the two men. They were both leaning back against the sofa, their legs spread in a relaxed pose, each sporting the bulge of an erection. The evidence of their arousal made her at once anxious and excited. At least they weren't bored or turned off.

Zach was smiling at her, his eyes hooded. Steve was staring at her with a disconcerting intensity that made her look away.

Keeping her eyes on Zach, Shea hooked her fingers into the elastic waist of her skirt and drew it down her legs. Kicking it away, she reached for her panties, her heart pounding a mile a minute. She pulled the lacey spandex fabric from her hips and let it slither down her legs.

Oh god, oh god, oh god, oh god, I'm naked. I'm naked in front of two men. Oh my god. What if I did it wrong? What if I look stupid?

She had done something in preparation for going to the club that she had never done in her life. It wasn't that she had planned for anyone to see—it was more that she thought, based on her research, it would put her in a better mindset, a submissive mindset, whatever that was.

She had bought a special emollient shaving cream made just for the bikini area and, first using scissors to remove the curls, and then a fresh razor, she had carefully denuded herself in the bathtub.

As she had examined herself in the mirror afterward, she had found the results startling. The cleft of her pussy was small, the outer labia framing it like a little pouch on either side. She had stroked her fingers along the smooth skin and then slipped them in between, surprised to find how wet and ready she was.

Still damp from her bath, she had lain on her bed and masturbated without even turning off the light. Without the overlay of pubic hair, the orgasm had been more intense, her fantasies fueled by her flying fingers, which became the fingers of her lover, her captor, her owner.

"Drop your hands to your sides and stand tall," Steve said, jerking her from her brief reverie.

Shea hadn't realized she had clasped her hands together in front of her torso, just below her breasts. She forced her fingers to release each other and let her arms fall to her sides. She pulled back her shoulders, aware this caused her breasts to thrust forward.

Zach rose from the couch. "A beautiful picture," he said with what sounded like genuine sincerity. "There's only one thing missing." He approached her, towering over her. He reached toward her throat.

Certain he was about to grip her below the jawline with thumb and forefinger, just like the secret rapist in her darkest fantasy, she emitted a small gasp and nearly took a step back. But his hand did not stop at her throat. Instead, he reached behind her neck and released the wide barrette that held back her hair.

At once, her unruly hair sprang around her face like a dozen of those toy coil-spring snakes hidden as a gag joke in pretend peanut jars. It took all Shea's self-control not to grab her hair up into a ponytail with both hands.

Speaking to Zach, Steve said enthusiastically, "Great hair. She should always leave it down. I bet we could braid it and use it as rope to tether her to the suspension rack. Wouldn't that be hot?"

As the vivid image he'd created whipped through her mind, Shea's hands lifted in spite of herself to at least tuck a few of the wild tendrils behind her ears, but Steve stopped her.

"No," he said sternly. "Leave your hands at your sides as you were directed."

Shea forced herself to obey him, clenching her hands into fists to keep them in place. She did surreptitiously try to blow an errant strand that had fallen over her eyes, but only succeeded in moving it further across her face.

Zach was still standing near her. "In this part of the interview," he said, "we will need to get a sense of your comfort level with nudity and with being handled and examined. If you decide to work with us for your submissive training, you need to be comfortable with our touching you in intimate and sexual ways. You will be required to perform various exercises and undergo training and discipline that you might find uncomfortable or embarrassing."

I already do find this uncomfortable and embarrassing, Shea thought but didn't say.

Zach continued, "It's obvious that you're not used to or comfortable with being naked in front of other people. Believe it or not, that particular issue will fall away pretty quickly once we really start training."

Easy for you to say, Shea wanted to reply, but did not. Instead, she tried to channel the submissives from the videos she liked to watch online. "Yes, Master Zach."

Zach grinned. "Master Zach, huh? It's a little soon for that, but if it makes you feel more comfortable, then by all means, you may call me Master Zach."

"And Sir Stephen," Shea blurted, shifting her gaze to the man still seated on the couch. Steve lifted one eyebrow, a sardonic expression on his face, as if to say, *"What, I don't rate Master?"*

Flustered, Shea explained, "Sir Stephen just sounds correct, don't you think?"

"Absolutely, S," Steve replied with a knowing smile.

Holy shit. He got the reference to O.

"The first physical exercise is easy," Zach said, pulling Shea's attention back to him. "I want you to place your hands behind your neck, fingers laced together, and spread your feet shoulder-width apart. I'm going to touch your body. I'm going to test your reaction to certain stimuli. Your job is very simple: remain still and in position with your hands behind your head. When I tell you to move or turn in a certain way, do exactly as I say and no more. Can you handle that, Shea?"

Shea tried to draw a breath to reply and found that her lungs had collapsed. She gave a small nod instead of answering as she reached beneath her heavy hair and entwined her fingers against the back of her head.

"Oh, and another thing," Zach continued as he stepped closer to her. "Now that you've introduced the concept of titles, going forward, when we are in this dungeon together, you will address me as Master Zach and you will call him"—he waved a hand back toward Steve—"Sir Stephen. When I ask you a question that requires an answer, you will answer the question using our titles, or Sir. Is that understood, Shea?"

Her lungs seemed to be functioning again. "Yes, Master Zach," she replied. "I understand."

"Good. Now turn around slowly until your back is facing the couch. You will not move again until you are directed to do so. You will not respond to anything we say unless you are expressly addressed. Is that clear?"

"Yes, Master Zach."

"Okay. Turn around."

Keeping her hands behind her neck, Shea turned in a half circle until her back was to the two men. She could feel their eyes raking over her body, lingering on her large ass and too-ample hips.

"That ass is perfect for spanking," Zach remarked from behind her.

"Oh, yeah," Steve agreed emphatically. "Her skin is so smooth and creamy. It will mark beautifully. I can't wait to whip her."

As if his words had ignited a pilot light deep in her belly, heat suddenly whooshed through Shea's body, perking her nipples into hard points and making her clit throb.

"I can't wait to whip her."

Oh my god, oh my god, oh my god.

She jumped when large, masculine hands cupped her ass cheeks. She recognized by his scent—soap and bay rum—that it was Zach behind her. He kneaded her cheeks and then drew his finger along the crack. It took every ounce of her self-will to remain still as he touched her in this intimate and unfamiliar way.

Finally Zach's hand fell away and he took a step back. "You're doing very well," he said from behind her. "I can sense this is hard for you."

You have no idea.

"Turn back around to face us," he continued. "Keep your hands behind your head."

Shea obeyed. As she turned to face them, Steve stood and approached her. He moved around her until he was standing just behind her. She could feel his body lightly pressed against her back and ass, barely touching her. She could smell his scent, different from Zach's, more spice and citrus and a certain male musk that made her nipples tingle.

She forgot about him as Zach reached for her breasts. He grasped her nipples between his thumbs and forefingers, rolling them until they were as hard as marbles. In spite of herself, Shea moaned softly at the pleasurable sensation and the thrill of her situation.

Then he twisted them suddenly, and a burst of pain hurtled through her nerve endings, making her cry out. Instinctively she took a step back, but Steve was behind her, blocking her movement. "Stay in position," he murmured in her ear, his voice deep and commanding.

Zach continued to twist her nipples, the pain nearly unbearable. Shea began to pant in her effort not to cry. Then Steve reached around her body and pressed his palm against her mons. He cupped the smooth skin, his fingers hooking between her legs and sliding into the slippery wet cleft.

Shea began to tremble, fear, pain and desire warring in the battlefield of her mind. The pain at Zach's hands and pleasure at Steve's tossed her like a Ping-Pong ball between them. This was both far better and far more terrible than her most intense masturbatory fantasy. Most importantly—it was real. These men were real, and not just figments of her dirty mind.

Then—all at once—as if they had planned it, both men stepped back, their hands falling away from her breasts and sex. Shea, who hadn't realized she'd closed her eyes, opened them in surprise. Her mouth, too, was hanging agape.

"Very nice," Zach said, something unreadable in his expression. "You're very responsive. That's an excellent trait in a submissive."

Steve appeared in front of her, his intense gaze on her as he lifted his fingers, the fingers that had been buried in her pussy just a moment before, to his nose. Closing his eyes, he inhaled deeply, a strange smile moving over his lips.

The blood pulsated into Shea's face as she whipped her head away.

"I agree with your assessment, Zach," she heard Steve say, though she couldn't bring herself to look at him again. "She's very responsive, but she's also uncomfortable with her body and her own reactions. Those are issues we would definitely need to work on if we decide to train this sub girl."

Shea couldn't deny the truth of his words. But it was the last phrase that really caught her attention: *if we decide to train this sub girl.* Until then she had thought it was all up to her. She had believed the interview, if that was what the hell this was, was being conducted so she could gain an understanding of what was being offered. Now she understood this was also a test. They might decide she wasn't proper sub material, not worthy of training.

The realization both stunned and galvanized her. If this was an audition, well then, she was going to get the part.

"Now it's time to assess your masochistic tendencies and tolerance levels," Steve said.

Finally Shea lifted her head. She saw that Zach had taken a seat on the couch.

"I already got a little sense of this during the brief spanking at the club," Steve said. "I'd like to take this opportunity to do a proper workup. Let's use the St. Andrew's cross. We'll start with a nice, sensual flogging." He held out his hand.

Lowering her arms, Shea placed her hand in his. His hand was cool and firm. Hers, by contrast, was sweaty with nerves. As they walked to the cross, she hoped she wouldn't make a fool of herself.

The cross was made of dark, polished wood with leather straps set at strategic intervals. "Lift your arms to the cuffs at the top of the X and stand with your feet shoulder-width apart," Steve instructed.

Shea did as she was told, extending her arms fully along the smooth wood. A jolt of excitement coursed through her body as he closed the leather and Velcro cuffs around each wrist. Though bondage had not figured largely in her fantasies, she couldn't deny the sweet, dark thrill of being held captive in this way, bound and at the mercy of another.

She swiveled her head to follow Steve as he walked away from her and toward a long rack filled with various whips, floggers, paddles and canes. He selected a very large flogger with dozens of long, thick leather tresses.

"This one is suede," he said as he ran the tresses through his fingers in a seductive way. "It doesn't sting as much as some of the others. I think you'll like it."

Shea tried to focus on his face instead of the huge flogger in his hands.

"For this exercise, I want you to close your eyes and relax. I want you to focus on the sensations of the leather against your skin. I know your safeword is zirconium. I don't expect you to use it, but I want you to know that I'm aware of it. This is really just an exercise. As I did with the spanking the other night, I'm going to start lightly and then slowly increase the intensity of my stroke. All I want you to do is accept the lash. Embrace whatever you're feeling. Don't try to censor yourself or stay quiet or tough your way through something that doesn't feel right."

He touched her shoulder. "You're doing really well so far."

"Thank you, Sir Stephen," she whispered, her heart hurtling against her ribcage.

He stepped behind her. Using both his hands, he massaged her shoulders, kneading away some of the bunched tension in her muscles. Then he leaned closer, his mouth near her ear. "Close your eyes. I'm going to whip you now, Shea."

She made an involuntary sound, something between a moan and a squeak. She closed her eyes.

The tresses landed lightly against her ass. They were soft, the stroke just a caress—it felt good. The second stroke landed a little harder, a slap of silky leather against her skin. He did this several times in a row, and Shea relaxed, un-curling her fingers and taking deep breaths to slow her rapidly beating heart.

The flogging began to intensify, the leather striking with a distinctive whacking sound that was at once arousing and unnerving. She was being whipped! It was like those online videos on the training site, except those weren't real, were they? This was real. Authentic. Maybe the most authentic thing she had ever done in her life.

He began to flog her up and down her back, stroking between her shoulder blades, thwacking her lower back, whipping in a stinging caress along her sides. Then came a thundering crash of leather against both ass cheeks.

Shea emitted a startled cry, her body tensing for another blow. It came quickly, a dozen stinging leather snakes striking her skin and leaving lines of fire in their wake. Sweat broke out on her upper lip and beneath her arms. Her heart was beating in triple time, her breathing ragged and uneven.

She felt a presence in front of her. Opening her eyes, she saw Zach standing there, his expression kind. He stroked her cheek, pushing the hair out of her face and tucking it behind her ears. "Slow your breathing," he counseled. "I want you to embrace the pain instead of fighting it. Take it inside of you. Make it a part of you."

Steve struck again, a stinging fury of tresses over the backs of her thighs. What the hell did that mean to embrace the pain, to make it a part of you? A human's natural instinct was to avoid pain. And yet, on some level, on the level that bypassed her intellect and training, Shea instinctively understood what Zach meant.

She managed to whisper breathlessly, "Yes, Master Zach."

The flogger moved up and down her back, the focus primarily on her ass. Each stroke was hard now, stinging against increasingly tender flesh. It hurt. Oh, oh, oh, it hurt. She wanted to be good and strong and brave, but it was too much. It was just too much.

"I can't," she cried suddenly. "It's too much."

"It's just enough," Steve said from behind her. "Five more, Shea. Take five more for me. I know you can do it."

Just five more.

Yes. She could do it.

The flogger exploded against her ass in a shower of pain. *One.*

She began to dance involuntarily, twisting her body in a vain effort to avoid the lash. *Two.*

Her safeword formed on her lips, but she pressed them together. She would not give up. *Three.*

"Ah!" she cried out as the flogger struck between her shoulder blades. *Four.*

The last stroke curled around her side, the tips cruelly striking her right breast. *Five.*

She was trembling from head to foot, tears rolling down her cheeks, her chest heaving. But something else was happening too—a kind of wild, crazy, careening joy was lifting her nearly off her feet.

This was it. This was what had been missing all her life. This moment, the stinging, perfect stroke of the leather, the cuffs embracing her wrists, keeping her centered, the heady scent of her own arousal mingled with bay rum, lime and male musk.

She was connected—she was alive—she was no longer alone.

As she came back to herself, she saw that Zach and Steve stood on either side of her, each reaching up to release a wrist cuff. When she staggered back, Zach caught her in his arms and helped her walk toward the couch. Instead of allowing her to sit, however, he pushed her gently to her stomach along the length of it.

They had draped a white sheet over the cushions, and the cotton was cool and smooth beneath her overheated, sweaty body.

"Just rest a few minutes," Zach said. "I'm going to smooth a little lotion onto your skin, more to relax you than anything. There are no marks, just some redness."

Steve approached, a tube of something and a small towel in his hand.

He crouched on the floor beside Zach. With a happy sigh, Shea closed her eyes as two pairs of masculine hands moved over her, spreading something soothing and fragrant into her skin.

"Did I pass the audition?" she murmured sleepily.

"With flying colors," Zach replied.

Chapter 4

"Wow, I didn't realize it was so late," Shea said, glancing at the wall clock over the kitchen sink. She and Steve were seated at the kitchen table, while Zach busied himself at the counter. Shea was again fully dressed, her hair pulled demurely back from her face.

Normally, they would have waited until a prospective trainee had left before making a decision about whether to take them on in a formal capacity, but this one was a no-brainer. As they'd rubbed salve into Shea's heated skin, they'd exchanged a look and a nod over the prone girl that had said it all—*let's do this*.

There was something about her—something so fresh and innocent, so completely without guile—that had captured Steve's full attention. Usually he went for the hardcore masochists with zero limits—but there was just something about Shea, something he was surprisingly eager to explore.

Zach came to the table, carrying three glasses. "Fresh OJ," he said. "Nothing better."

"Thanks," Shea said, accepting a glass. "I am thirsty."

Zach handed Steve his and took a seat at the table. Lifting his glass to his lips, Zach swallowed the entire contents in one long gulp.

Steve, cupping his cold glass in both hands, watched Shea as she sipped her juice. She was staring into the middle distance, a dreamy expression on her face—the rosy, unfocused look of a satisfied lover, or, more accurately in this case, a well-used sub girl. She seemed lost in a daze, and Steve found himself wondering just what she was thinking about, but he didn't want to disturb her reverie to find out.

"So, Shea," Zach said, startling both Steve and Shea with his big, powerful baritone. "Let's talk a little about what you experienced tonight. You clearly had a powerful reaction to the flogging. Is it what you were expecting?"

Shea blinked several times. The dreamy look faded as she focused on Zach's face. "It was a fascinating experiment," she replied in a professorial manner. She closed her eyes a moment as if retrieving data. Opening them again, she said, "The DSM-IV defines masochism as when the individual experiences recurrent, intense sexually arousing fantasies, sexual urges, or behaviors involving the act of being humiliated, beaten, bound, or otherwise made to suffer.

"I've always had trouble with that concept, even though I was undeniably attracted to BDSM. Especially when you add in the concept of sexual submission. I mean"—she looked from Zach to Steve, lifting her hands, palms up, for emphasis—"how do you reconcile conscious subjugation of your will—allowing yourself to become the passive object of another—with feminism and self-actualization? I'm just as good as, or better than, any man in my field, and yet...and yet the idea of erotic submission, the thrill of it, the *rightness* of it—I can't deny it. Not after meeting the two of you. Not after what you've shown me so far."

"I don't know about all that," Zach said with a shrug. "Seems to me what matters is how you actually feel, not how you think you're *supposed* to feel."

"I agree with Zach," Steve said. "I don't think there's a conflict here, Shea, not once you get past all the fancy language." While amused she had slipped once more behind her intellectual shield, he didn't want her to retreat there for too long. "Submission is the very antithesis of passivity. In fact, it's a supreme act of courage. What you did tonight— baring yourself for us—not only your body, but your fears and desires— and allowing yourself to be bound and flogged—that wasn't the action of a passive, timid person. It was a courageous act. I know I speak for both of us when I say we're very impressed with what we've seen so far."

He glanced toward Zach, who nodded enthusiastically. "I guess the question now is, would you like to continue with us? Are you interested in more formalized training with Zach and me?"

The shining light had returned to Shea's blue eyes. As he stared into them, Steve noticed the irises were ringed with gold. They were the most extraordinary eyes he had ever seen. He held his breath as he waited for her to answer, as he silently willed her to consent.

Shea didn't keep them in suspense. "Oh, yes!" she exclaimed eagerly. Then, looking slightly embarrassed, she added in a softer tone, "Yes, please."

"Hey, that's great," Zach said with such exuberance Steve had to smile. "Why don't you text us tomorrow and we'll figure out a schedule, okay?"

"Sounds good," Shea agreed with a smile.

"Good." Steve held up his glass. "To new adventures," he said with a grin.

"Thank you," Shea said. "Thanks for this chance." She lifted her glass to touch his and then ducked her head as color began to seep over her cheeks. Setting down her glass, she pushed back in her chair and stood. Zach and Steve rose along with her.

"Do you know the way from here?" Zach asked as they walked her out through the garage and to her car.

"I'll GPS it," Shea said, holding up her phone. "Thank goodness for this thing. I get lost on the way to my apartment parking lot." She clicked her key fob to unlock her car door. "Thanks again for tonight," she said, looking first at Zach and then at Steve. "It was"—she paused, as if searching for the right word—"amazing."

"You were great," Zach said enthusiastically. "Next time," he added, "be ready for anything."

~*~

As they had been that night at Hardcore, the guys were wearing black leather pants and boots. Shea liked the contrast of Steve's sun-streaked blond hair and very blue eyes against the silky black of his button-down shirt, the sleeves rolled up on his forearms, the top unbuttoned at the throat to reveal his smooth, tan chest. He was at once elegant and devastatingly sexy. Zach wore only an open black leather vest, perfectly tailored over his broad back and shoulders. He had luxuriant, dark curling chest hair that tapered down past rippling abs, drawing her eye to his bulging crotch. The guy could have been a cover model for a romance novel.

"Uh-uh." Steve placed a restraining hand on Shea's shoulder as she started to enter the dungeon. "Trainees strip at the door unless otherwise directed."

Shea froze. Yes, of course she knew she'd have to get naked again, but hadn't realized it would be right off the bat. At least she would get to control the order of clothing removal this time.

It was seven o'clock on Wednesday evening, and Shea had spent every waking and most of her sleeping hours since she'd left their dungeon on Monday night anticipating this moment. She'd been too jittery to eat much, not even the hidden stashes of ice cream and cookies she kept on hand for emergencies. She had been subsisting on coffee and apples, her stomach tied in knots.

Work had actually been a saving grace—giving her something to focus on so she wouldn't jump out of her skin with nerves as she veered between thrilled excitement and dubious anxiety about what she was signing up for. She'd come in very early and stayed late, so now she was actually ahead of the game—her big project completed, save for some last tweaks to the formulation.

She'd left work that afternoon at five, ignoring Jeff's sarcastic comment of, "Where you headed off to in such a rush? Got a big date?" and then his guffawing laugh, as if such a thing were remote in the extreme. Imagine his shock if he knew where she was actually going?

She'd taken a long shower, carefully grooming every inch of her body and deep conditioning her hair. It had taken her forever to select an outfit, the entire contents of her wardrobe scattered across her bed by the time she was done. In the end, she chose the first thing she'd put on—a pair of tailored black pants that a salesperson had once assured her gave her a slim line, and a simple cream-colored button-down blouse so she wouldn't have to pull anything over her head. She'd even sprung for a second lacy bra and panties set at Victoria's Secret during her lunch break the day before, spending way more than she should have on a sexy push-up bra that made her breasts look like two cantaloupes on a plate, but which the saleslady had assured her would be the envy of every woman and the object of lust of every man in any room she walked into.

Shea wasn't entirely comfortable at the thought of being such an object of scrutiny, until she reminded herself the only room she'd be walking into in this bra was Zach and Steve's dungeon.

Master Zach and Sir Stephen.

She'd masturbated herself to sleep Monday and Tuesday night with those words on her lips, as wild, new scenarios involving the two guys superseded her old and, she now realized, much worn previous erotic fantasies.

"Fold your clothing neatly and place it in the cubbies there beside the door," Steve continued, pointing to a tall, narrow shelf comprised of four wooden cubes stacked one on top of the other. "You can leave your purse there, too. Oh, that reminds me," he added. "Did you bring your medical record?"

Shea reached into her bag and pulled out the envelope with the copy of her last physical and the results of her most recent comprehensive blood work. When they'd scheduled the session, they'd asked if she could bring what she had. She understood this was a natural precaution, and indeed, approved of it. After all, they were going to touch her in intimate ways—the thought sent a tremor of thrilled terror and delight through her—and they needed to know she was healthy and not somehow contagious.

Steve took the envelope and opened it, while Zach, who had already entered the dungeon ahead of them, handed Shea two pieces of paper. She took the pages, which were printed on official-looking stationary from a doctor's office and attested to Zach's and Steve's clean bills of health.

Barely able to focus on the information, she gave it a cursory glance and handed the pages back to Zach, aware she could no longer put off the inevitable. After placing her purse in the top cubby, she slipped out of her flats and put them in the bottom cubby.

She took a deep, cleansing breath and blew it out slowly. Reminding herself they'd already seen her naked and hadn't run screaming for the hills, she slowly unbuttoned her blouse. Before taking it all the way off, however, she unzipped her pants to eliminate any possible fat roll issue.

She removed the blouse, letting it fall from her shoulders, both pleased and slightly alarmed by their admiring, openly lustful gazes at her breasts, lifted and offered in very expensive satin and lace cut so low it barely covered her nipples. Hands only trembling slightly, she folded the blouse and placed it carefully in the cubby just below her purse.

Next came the pants, which she pushed down her legs, trying to suck in her gut as much as possible as she bent forward and stepped out of them. She put them on top of the blouse and turned again to face the guys.

"Bra and panties," Steve said brusquely. "And that barrette thing, too. We will put your hair up as necessary during bondage, but that will be our decision."

Bondage.

A shiver of anticipation moved through Shea as she reached for her barrette and released the catch that held it closed. She ran her fingers through her thick, unruly hair and tried to push it away from her face, but then gave up. At least it was shiny and clean. She placed the barrette beside her purse.

Finally, and again reminding herself they'd already seen the worst, she reached back and unclasped her bra, letting it fall forward as she slipped the satin straps from her shoulders. Her heavy breasts bounced free.

Her mouth was dry, her tongue sticking to the roof of her mouth as she tried to swallow. Heart pounding, she pushed the tiny panties down her legs. With trembling hands, she shoved her underthings into a cubby. Finally turning to face the trainers, she tried to breathe, aware her face was turning tomato-red as heat washed over her cheeks like scalding water.

"It's okay, Shea," Zach said, his expression at once kind and amused. "We're not going to eat you up, I promise."

"Nudity is a part of submission," Steve added. "It's a demonstration of your willingness to offer yourself without barriers, without placing obstacles like clothing between you and your trainers. This shyness of yours will definitely be a focus in your initial training. You will learn quickly that modesty has no place in a D/s relationship."

D/s relationship.

Dominance and submission.

Just the words sent a jolt of fear and desire through Shea. The R word was another matter, but she understood he meant the relationship of a trainer and sub, nothing more.

Intellectually, she appreciated Steve's comment about modesty and no barriers. And if she were a size six, or even a size ten, she was sure she'd be a lot more comfortable with the whole concept of nudity. There was no getting around it—things were easier for the skinny girls. They breezed through life, everything good handed to them on a platter. This injustice made her think about Oreos, but, to her surprise, she didn't even want one.

She wanted to be here, doing this, as hard as it was, as scary as it was.

"Come on over to the kneeling pad," Master Zach said, gesturing for her to follow them to the mat in front of the couch.

They took their seats on the sofa in the same positions as on Monday night, while Shea stepped onto the black mat.

"Get on your knees," Sir Stephen commanded. "Back straight, hands resting on your thighs, chin up."

Shea hesitated, wondering if she'd looked fatter standing or kneeling. *Stop it,* she ordered herself. *Do as you're told.*

With their eyes on her, she lowered herself as gracefully she could to the mat and placed her hands on her thighs.

"Spread your knees wider," Sir Stephen said. "Show us your cunt."

Heat spread yet again over Shea's cheeks, moving down her throat and up through the roots of her hair. Their casual use of the word *cunt* still startled her, though it didn't offend her. While she didn't like when men used the word as an epithet to put a woman down, she secretly liked the term better than pussy for her private parts.

Cunt was so earthy, so immediate, so...sexual.

Liking the word was one thing—being asked to expose herself like that in front of the two fully-clothed men was quite another.

Modesty has no place in a D/s relationship.

They were both boring holes into her with their eyes. While Master Zach's expression was patient, if amused, Sir Stephen's gaze was like a laser, probing into all her deepest secrets.

Determined to obey, Shea forced her knees to spread until her denuded pussy—her *cunt*—was exposed to their scrutiny.

Master Zach leaned forward, his hands on his knees. "So, from our time together so far," he said, "we've learned you're masochistic and crave erotic pain, but we don't have a real sense of your submissive tendencies. I guess my first question would be, what does being submissive mean to you? Is it just allowing yourself to be tied up and whipped, or is there more at play for you?" He let his gaze move slowly down her body, his eyes hooding as he stared at her shaven, exposed cunt.

Her face hot, Shea glanced from Master Zach to Sir Stephen. His eyes were fixed on her face as he regarded her with an intense, narrow-eyed gaze, as if he were reading and weighing her thoughts.

Shea struggled to pick the right words from the jumble in her mind. Finally drawing on her research, she said, "I know submission is also about obedience and service. It's about relinquishing control. It's about giving yourself fully to your Master, without reservation."

"Okay," Master Zach said. "And what does it mean for *you*? Just say whatever pops into your head—forget about what you think we expect. When you hear the words *obedience, service, control*, how does that make you feel?"

"Sexy," Shea admitted. "Excited. Vulnerable. Scared." Her nipples tingled, and though she didn't look down, she knew they were jutting forward like gumdrops.

"Go on," Master Zach urged gently. "Imagine yourself tied down, rope wrapped tightly around your body, binding your wrists, your ankles, your thighs, your breasts. You aren't resisting, or blushing, or thinking anything at all except how you can please your Master—how you can suffer for his pleasure, submit to his commands. You're exposed, your legs spread wide, your cunt offered for your Master's whip, or his kiss, or his cock..."

"Oh," Shea whispered, the word yanked from her by the picture he painted. Her cunt felt swollen, her clit throbbing.

"Do you want that, Shea?" Master Zach murmured, his voice low and throaty. "Are you prepared to do whatever it takes to get to that place?"

"Yes," Shea managed, her voice suddenly hoarse, though in fact she had no idea if she was up to the challenge, or what it truly entailed. She cleared her throat and repeated, "Yes. Yes, please, Master Zach."

He smiled, the playfulness she'd grown used to in his grin no longer there, replaced by something harder and infinitely sexier.

Sir Stephen, his eyes still on Shea's face, said quietly, "Fantasy is one thing, Shea. Reality is quite another. We will put you to the test, but remember, there is no failure, only a learning curve we expect you to climb. We will both encourage and correct you as needed as we move further into the process."

"Yes, Sir," she whispered. She wished the interview would end—though terrified, she was also longing for what they offered. She was ready for that promised rope. She'd been waiting a lifetime.

"Normally at this early stage in a sub's training," Sir Stephen continued, "we would discuss your hard limits and your goals, but I'm guessing you don't really know yourself at this point. Would you agree?"

"Yes, Sir. Completely," Shea blurted, relief and gratitude flooding her at the realization he was taking control—no more questions, no more probing into thoughts and fantasies she could barely articulate, even to herself.

The two Doms exchanged a glance and then both rose to their feet. Sir Stephen leaned down and tapped Shea's shoulder. "That tap on the shoulder indicates release from whatever position you are in, and is your cue to stand."

Shea got to her feet, and the guys led her to the bondage table, which was set on four thick, sturdy legs. Approximately three feet wide and eight feet long, it was covered in black leather, metal rings embedded around the perimeter of the thickly padded tabletop.

Master Zach reached beneath the table and brought up a triangular pillow wedge wrapped in a black cotton pillowcase. "Lie down on your back on the table, and then I'm going to put this under your ass," he instructed.

Shea sat on the edge of the table and then maneuvered herself back so she was lying down as instructed. She was relieved to be lying down, as her legs had turned to rubber as they'd led her to the table.

"Lift your ass," Master Zach instructed, nudging at her thigh with the pillow wedge. Shea obeyed, and Master Zach slid the pillow beneath her, which forced her pelvis up higher than the rest of her body.

Sir Stephen produced several hanks of thick rope that had been dyed a rich, deep red. "Sometimes we just use cuffs, but for today's exercise, I want you to feel the rope."

He unwrapped a hank of rope and wound it around her right wrist. He knotted it in place and took the free end, which he wrapped around one of the rings at the head of the table, adjusting it until her arm was fully extended over her head. He did the same with her second wrist until both arms were completely immobilized.

"How does that feel?" he asked, tugging gently at one of the ropes. "Too tight? Too loose?"

Shea pulled at the restraints. "It's good, Sir," she breathed, stunned at the *rightness* of the smooth, supple rope against her skin.

Master Zach, standing at the base of the table, wrapped and knotted rope around her ankles, tying them off to rings on either side of the table so her legs were spread wide, her naked cunt raised by the wedge and on full display. She was completely helpless at the hands of these two men she barely knew, but somehow instinctively trusted. The feeling was at once terrifying and more thrilling than any she'd ever known.

"Sweet," Master Zach said, drawing out the word, his eyes glittering as he stared down at her.

"But it needs something more," Sir Stephen said from her other side. Bending down, he reached beneath the table and produced another hank of rope, also dyed red, but thinner. This he wrapped around Shea's breasts, winding it in a tight figure eight, bunching them together so they stood like cherry-topped mounds on her chest. She could feel the pressure building in her breast tissue. It was both incredibly erotic and a little scary.

Sir Stephen leaned down and spoke softly into her ear. "You're at our mercy now, Shea. How does it feel?"

"Perfect, Sir," she blurted before she could stop herself. But why should she stop herself? It was true.

He smiled, a wicked smile that sent a jolt of icy, delicious fear through her veins. "Good. That's just how it should feel. Now, we're going to test your sexual responsiveness. The only thing you need to remember is to ask for permission to come, as, while you're in this dungeon, we own your orgasms. Is that clear?"

Shea's heart, which had already been beating plenty fast, began to hammer violently in her chest. Was now when she admitted just how little experience she actually had? She opened her mouth to confess, but no words came. It was too late to back out now, and really, beyond the fear and uncertainty, the desire was welling inside her, rising like a wave she could no longer, and no longer wanted to, resist.

All she could do was nod.

~*~

Christ, she was gorgeous lying there with her hair tumbling around her face in a riot of red against the rich black leather of the bondage table. Her cheeks were flushed, her nipples dark pink and fully distended. Her breasts, bound in the tight rope, were also darkening with trapped blood, though he'd been careful not to tie them so tightly as to cut off circulation. Steve could smell the heady, rich scent of female arousal, and his mouth actually watered at the thought of tasting her.

But what he loved most was the fear in her eyes—the helpless, pleading look that made his balls ache and his cock throb. As he stared down at Shea, naked and bound in all her voluptuous beauty, he had to restrain himself from climbing on top of her and entering her with a single, savage thrust.

He did no such thing, of course, and not just because Zach was standing at the other end of the table. Shea was not there as his toy, he reminded himself sternly, but as his trainee, as their trainee. They were testing her sexual responsiveness so they could better design her training program. He was a professional.

Yeah, keep telling yourself that.

Fortunately, Zach was on the case, which gave Steve a chance to get himself under control. It was good they'd agreed in advance that Zach would be the one to stimulate her, since Steve still wasn't sure he could have controlled himself.

Zach stood at the end of the table between Shea's spread legs, holding the tube of lubricant he'd pulled from the storage bin they kept beneath the bondage table. He pushed up the plastic lid and squirted some gel onto his fingers. Setting the tube aside, he leaned forward and lightly stroked the dark pink petals of her labia while Steve looked on.

Shea closed her eyes and moaned, the sound low and feral.

Zach and Steve exchanged a glance, silently communicating their approval. Zach continued to stroke and tease her until she began to tremble, her eyes squeezed tightly shut, her hands clenched into fists overhead.

Steve tapped her fists with his index fingers. "Relax your hands. Fists are a sign of resistance."

Shea's eyes opened and she stared up at him with apparent incomprehension.

"Relax." He tapped her fists again, and this time they slowly unfurled.

Satisfied, Steve glanced again at Zach, who gave a nod. Taking two fingers, Zach pushed them slowly into Shea's cunt.

Shea jerked hard against her restraints as she emitted a startled yelp.

Zach, his fingers still inside her, soothed, "Take it easy, Shea. It's all good. You're doing great."

She fixed a wild-eyed gaze on Steve, who bent over her with some concern. "What's the matter? Is he hurting you?"

She shook her head and moved her lips, as if trying to speak, but no sound came, save for a groan that ended in a sigh as her eyes fluttered shut once more.

Glancing back at Zach, Steve saw he was moving his fingers inside the girl, no doubt stimulating her G-spot, based on her reaction.

Using his other hand, Zach rubbed two fingers in a circle over and around Shea's clit while he continued to finger-fuck her. Shea began to tremble again, her entire body shuddering as she moaned and pulled against the ropes that held her down.

Jesus, was she going to come already? Steve allowed himself a chuckle—the shy ones were so often the most responsive, and Shea was no exception.

"Permission," he reminded her, leaning down. "You must ask for permission."

"Please!" she cried, bucking now against her restraints as Zach relentlessly stroked and frigged her. "Can I, oh, god, oh, yes, please, can I cooo…" The incomplete word rolled into another low, throaty moan, followed by a series of agitated yips.

Zach let his hands fall away, which produced a series of aftershocks in the bound, naked girl. "Oops," he said, grinning at Steve. "I think we have a naughty girl on our hands. Someone came before they had permission."

Shea's eyes flew open, and Steve knew, if her hands had been free, they would have flown to her mouth. "Oh, Sir!" she cried. "I tried to ask. I did. It just, I don't know, it swept over me. I've never experienced *anything* like that in my life."

Something in her expression and the fervent tone of her words drew Steve up a little short. "Anything?" he echoed, staring down at her to read her face. "Are you saying that's the most powerful orgasm you've ever had at the hands of another?"

The girl, who seemed to have an endless capacity to blush, turned scarlet as she mumbled something he couldn't understand.

"What's that?" he said more sharply than he'd intended. "Speak up."

"I said," she replied, though it was clearly hard for her to say the words. "That's the *first* orgasm I've ever had at the hands of another, Sir."

Wait.

What?

CHAPTER 5

It was on the tip of Steve's tongue to demand further explanation, but something in Zach's expression, along with the slight shake of his head, told Steve to wait. As he released Shea from her restraints and helped her to a sitting position, Steve recognized that Zach was correct, as usual. Better to keep the momentum of the session going. There was time later to delve into Shea's sexual experience, or lack thereof.

As he unwound the ropes from her breasts, he informed her, "You came without permission, and that calls for punishment."

"Punishment...Sir?" Shea murmured, the dismay evident on her face.

Steve nodded. "Don't add to your infractions by questioning me, S."

Shea slapped her hand against her mouth with almost comical alacrity.

By making her wait until the end of the session for her punishment, her anticipation would build, along with her anxiety and arousal. Such was the predicament of a masochist. Thinking about this gave Steve an idea. "Before your punishment, we're going to have a lesson in anticipation. I want you to lie down again. Place your arms at your sides and bend your knees so your feet are flat against the table. During this exercise, you're free to cry out, but you may not lift your hands to stop us, or impede us in any way. Are we clear, so far?"

Shea swallowed visibly, but nodded as she replied, "Yes, Sir Stephen."

"Your main goal in this exercise," Zach said, picking up the thread, "is to accept what's given to you without trying to anticipate or resist it in any way. You're working on acceptance—on taking what your Dom gives you without trying to control or top from the bottom."

"That means you don't tense up or flinch or wince or protest," Steve continued. "You accept what we give you. All you have to do is lie there and take it."

He could almost hear her unspoken thought—*Easy for you to say*—as the emotions flickered over her face, but she said nothing.

Steve turned to Zach. "You want to select your toys first?"

With a nod, Zach went to the supply counter, returning a second later with a black satin sleep mask and a pair of black leather gloves. Not just any gloves, these were one of Taggart Fitzgerald's most popular custom pieces. The lined leather hid the prickly metal points embedded between the layers at strategic spots in the palms and fingertips. It was an excellent tool for sensation play, its touch sharp enough to elicit a gasp and leave a mark, but not so sharp as to cut the skin.

Zach handed the mask to Steve and then pulled on the gloves while Shea watched with wide eyes. "I think you'll like these gloves," Zach said. "They're special." He drew a gloved finger over the surface of her right breast, leaving a faint pink mark in its wake and pulling a gasp of startled surprise from the girl's lips.

"Things aren't always what they seem," Steve murmured. "We'll be exposing you to a number of different sensations during this exercise." He held out the sleep mask. "To help you focus, you'll be blindfolded.

We want you to fully experience all the sensations without trying to anticipate them. Just accept what is given to you," he reiterated as he slipped the mask into place over her eyes. "Can you do that, S?"

"I hope so, Sir," she replied in a slightly tremulous voice.

Steve placed his thumb and forefinger just below her jawline and applied enough pressure to get her attention.

She gasped, her hands nearly lifting from the table, though she managed to stop herself in time.

"That response is not good enough in this dungeon," Steve corrected her. "Answer the question with a yes or a no."

A tremor rippled through her body, her nipples stiffening to erect points at the center of each breast, his grip on her throat clearly a powerful trigger. "Yes," she managed. "Yes, Sir Stephen. I can do that."

Satisfied, he released her throat and took a step back. He nodded toward Zach, who placed his gloved hands lightly over both of Shea's breasts. Zach began to move his hands along her body as Steve stepped over to the supply counter to get what he needed.

He returned with a candle, a box of matches, a single tail whip, a small bowl of ice cubes and a feather duster.

As Zach moved his hands down Shea's abdomen, he left pale pink scratches on her skin. She was doing an admirable job of remaining still, though her hands, Steve now noted, were curled into fists.

Using the handle of the single tail, he tapped at each fist in turn. "Uncurl your fingers," he commanded. "Open yourself to what's happening to you."

After several seconds, Shea finally obeyed, letting her hands fall open at her sides.

Steve reached for her throat, catching her again just below the jawline.

Shea jerked at his touch and cried out.

Without removing his hand, he said, "You can do better, S. When either of us gives you a command, you obey instantly, not in your own sweet time." To emphasize the point, he grabbed the single tail with his other hand and struck her right breast.

Shea gasped in pain, her fingers twitching, but, to her credit, she managed to keep her arms at her sides.

The sight of the welt, first white and then flushing to an angry red across the top of her right breast, made Steve's cock hard as a rock. He briefly fantasized about pulling her forward so her head dangled from the edge of the table and thrusting his cock deep into her throat. Well aware that this went far beyond the parameters of basic submissive training, he kept himself under control.

Steve set down the single tail and picked up the candle and the box of matches. "Open your knees wider," he ordered the sub. "Show us your cunt."

With a tremulous sigh, Shea did as she was commanded.

Zach touched his spiked fingertips to Shea's cunt while Steve lit the candle. Shea moaned as Zach began to move his fingers in a circular pattern against her labia and clit.

Steve held the candle over her breasts. Shea squealed as the first hot drops of melted wax splashed against her flesh. Steve reached for a piece of ice and ran it along the welt he had placed there a moment before. Shea shuddered and drew in a sharp, gasping breath.

Zach reached for the single tail with his left hand, while still stroking Shea's clit with his right, his fingers now angled in such a way that the spikes were not involved.

Shea moaned like an animal in heat, the scent of her musk hanging in the air like an aphrodisiac.

All at once, Zach withdrew his gloved hand and let the single tail snap, albeit lightly, against the girl's spread pussy.

With a cry, Shea slammed her legs closed, her hands coming up in front of her body as if to ward off an attack.

"That's another infraction," Steve said sternly. "How dare you raise your hands to us? Put them at your sides and open your legs. Now."

Shea was panting, her body trembling. Zach and Steve exchanged a look—it was possible they were moving too quickly, and she would fail the exercise, but Steve didn't think so. Shea O'Connor, despite her innocence and her lack of experience, had that special kind of submissive courage that would allow her to get through this, if only she could dig deep enough within herself to harness it. Steve waited, silently willing her to succeed.

She dropped her arms back to the padded table and parted her legs, exposing her pussy once more without knowledge of what might, or might not, come next.

Zach and Steve smiled at one another. Then Zach flicked the whip in the air just beside her thigh. Shea flinched and gasped, her knees again closing like a gate.

"Stop anticipating," Steve reminded her sharply. "Back into position."

"I don't know if I can, Sir," Shea gasped. "You're scaring me."

"Work through the fear," Zach said in his deep, gentle voice. "That's a part of submission. Harness your fear and let it make you strong."

Again Shea opened her knees, and again Zach snapped the whip in the air. This time, though she startled, Shea managed to maintain her position. Zach and Steve exchanged a glance of approval. She was a quick learner, and clearly she was trying her best to obey.

They alternated without any discernable pattern so she would stop trying to anticipate as they splashed hot droplets of wax over her skin, or stroked her breasts and inner thighs with the feather duster and the texture gloves, or drew ice over heated flesh marked by the single tail.

They stimulated, tortured, stroked and teased her until at last she stopped clenching her fists, bunching her muscles or flinching with anticipation. Only when she lay completely still and open to them, her mouth slack, her body sheened with sweat, her hair a wild torrent around her face, did they relent.

Finally, Zach removed the mask, and Shea blinked up at him as she focused. "Hey," he said softly. "You did great. How're you doing?"

"Wonderful, Sir," she breathed with such fervent sincerity that both Zach and Steve laughed with delight.

~*~

Zach's cock was so hard that its outline was completely visible against the soft leather of his pants. He couldn't remember working with such a responsive, sensitive submissive. While he'd enjoyed the anticipation exercise, he'd especially loved bringing Shea to such a powerful orgasm.

The way she had shuddered and moaned as he'd stroked her sopping wet cunt had made him feel not only as powerful as a god but also oddly protective, as if he were the lifeline that kept her tethered to the earth, as if only he could keep her safe at the same time as he pushed her over the edge.

Steve assisted Shea to a sitting position and Zach helped her from the table, steadying her as her feet touched the floor.

"Now," Steve said, "It's time for your punishment."

As if suddenly aware of her nudity, Shea placed one arm across her breasts, the other at an angle over her stomach and crotch.

"Hands at your side," Zach reminded her.

"What do you think, Zach," Steve said, "Shall we put her on the punishment brick?"

"I think that's a great idea," Zach replied.

"The punishment brick, Sir?" Shea echoed in a squeak.

"Do you have a specific question, S?" Steve asked with an arch of his eyebrow.

She looked from him to Zach and then back to Steve. "Uh, no Sir," she managed.

Good girl. She was learning.

They led her to the punishment corner, where chains hung from the ceiling, cuffs dangling at their ends. Zach pulled one of the large cement bricks they kept for this purpose from its place against the wall and set it beneath the chains. He helped Shea step up onto the brick, keeping his hands on her waist as she struggled to find her balance. The brick was about twenty-two inches long and fifteen inches wide, its surface rough against bare feet.

Steve, meanwhile, brought over a small stepladder. Climbing up, he reached to adjust the chains to the proper height. "Lift your arms over your head," he directed Shea. "I'm going to cuff your wrists. Make sure you keep your feet firmly on the block, or you'll find yourself dangling off the ground."

She cast Zach one last pleading glance before lifting her arms over her head.

You can do it, he urged silently, offering an encouraging smile.

Steve wrapped the cuffs snugly around each of her wrists and then adjusted the chains to pull her arms taut overhead. Shea shifted precariously on the brick, executing an involuntary little dance as she found her footing once more.

As Zach replaced the stepladder against the wall, Steve went to the supply cabinet and returned with a pair of clover clamps and a soft fabric gag. He handed the gag to Zach and then held up the clamps for Shea to see. "Do you know what these are, S?" Steve asked.

Though he felt almost sorry for Shea, Zach couldn't deny his arousal. He loved a good punishment. And after all, she did need correction.

Shea stared at the nipple clamps and slowly nodded, catching her lower lip in her teeth.

"Answer the question," Steve snapped.

"Yes, Sir Stephen," she managed. "They're nipple clamps. Clover clamps, to be precise," she added in what Zach was already coming to think of as her professor voice. "They were invented in Japan. They have a unique property in that, the more the clamps are pulled on, the tighter they squeeze."

Steve lifted his eyebrows and flashed Zach a quick look of amusement. Zach didn't try to hide his answering grin.

Turning back to Shea, Steve asked, "Have you ever experienced nipple clamps, S?"

"No, Sir," she replied, her voice now a whisper.

"Remember what they feel like next time you think about coming without permission." Steve gripped her right nipple and tugged at it. He opened one of the clamps and placed it over the base of her nipple.

He let it spring closed and, predictably, Shea gave a yelp of pain, jerking back and nearly losing her balance on the brick in the process.

Ignoring her, Steve reached for her other nipple, expertly sliding the second clamp into place. Again, Shea cried out, though this time she managed to remain still. "Oh, god," she moaned softly. "It hurts. It really, really hurts, Sir."

Steve's smile was cruel. "Of course it does. That's the point."

He pulled lightly against the chain. Shea whimpered. A thin sheen of sweat had broken out on her upper lip, and her chest was heaving.

Zach stepped closer to the girl and pushed the hair from her face. "Slow your breathing," he advised her. "The pain will lessen as your nipples numb. Accept this punishment with grace, Shea. You can do it."

He waited until she gave a small nod, and then continued, "During punishments, we expect you to exercise self-discipline. That means you don't cry out." He held up the gag. "Because this is your first punishment, we'll use a gag to help you stay quiet. When you feel the need to scream, just bite down on it."

"To scream..." Shea echoed faintly. Swallowing hard, she whispered, "What about my safeword? Should I use a hand gesture if I need to?" She was trembling now, and Zach worried they might be moving too fast.

Apparently similarly concerned, Steve said, "Take her temperature."

Zach nodded and reached between Shea's legs. She gasped as his fingers slid over her labia. She was soaking wet, her clit a small, hard pea against his fingertip.

His hand still against her heat, Zach met Steve's eyes. "On fire," he announced with a grin.

Steve nodded, satisfied. It was only with reluctance that Zach let his hand fall away.

"In answer to your question," Steve continued, "if you think you need to use your safeword, yes, use a hand gesture. Just open and close your hands, like this." He demonstrated with his hands. "We will be paying attention. But be aware—a safeword is a last resort in the scene. You don't use it because something hurts or because you're scared. The only time a safeword should be used is when not using it is simply not an option. An example would be if you're certain that your Doms are not paying attention to your needs, or your body, or the signals you are giving them."

"If you use your safeword," Zach added, "the session will end—there's no going back. Everything will stop. We're not saying you can never use your safeword. We just want you to understand it's for true emergencies."

"That's right," Steve said. "Zach and I pride ourselves on the fact we have never had a sub use her safeword during training. Though it may not seem like it, we are constantly assessing what you can handle and when we need to pull back. I know it's early in the training, but you need to trust us. We know what we're doing." He let that sink in a moment, and then said, "So, are you ready to proceed with your punishment?"

Shea let out a deep breath and then replied, "Yes, Sir Stephen."

Steve moved to stand behind her while Zach twisted the strip of fabric and touched the center of it to Shea's lips. When she opened her mouth, he pushed it between her teeth and handed the two ends to Steve, who tied them into a knot behind her head.

She looked incredibly hot, her eyes wide with fear, and also with desire. He loved the vivid, erotic tableau of the naked, suspended girl, with her tousled, long hair, the white cloth between her lips and those rosy pink nipples caught in the silver clamps.

Steve retrieved a large wooden punishment paddle from the whip rack and held it up for Shea to see. "Twenty whacks. Remember, not a sound."

Shea blinked rapidly, as if to blink back tears, but she nodded her agreement.

As Steve stepped behind the girl, Zach reached for her face, cupping her hot cheeks with his hands. "Show us your courage, Shea. You can do this." He stared into her eyes, resisting a sudden impulse to kiss her.

The paddle made a delicious whacking sound as it met her flesh. "One," Steve pronounced.

A muffled whimper escaped the gag, more of surprise, Zach thought, than pain.

Steve struck her again. "Two."

Shea jerked in her restraints, nearly losing her footing as she danced on the concrete brick. She managed to remain silent, though her eyes were wide, her nostrils flared.

"Keep your eyes on mine," Zach said. "Draw your strength from me. Take what's coming to you."

Steve struck her again, the full force of the unforgiving wooden paddle crashing against her ass. Zach, a firm believer in experiencing everything he expected his sub to endure, knew firsthand just how much a paddle could hurt. There was nothing sensual about it—no soothing stroke of soft leather or warming tap of a cane. It was a punishment, pure and simple, and Shea would have the bruises to prove it.

Steve struck her again and again, each blow of the paddle like fingers fondling Zach's cock and balls. Through it all, he cupped Shea's face in support, sending her strength and encouragement with his gaze.

"You're doing good," he urged. "Almost done."

When Steve finally intoned, "Twenty," Shea's face was streaked with tears and she was trembling like a leaf in the wind, the chain swaying between her breasts.

Steve set down the paddle and reached for the knot behind her head. Letting go of her face, Zach plucked the saliva-soaked fabric from her mouth and tucked it into his back pocket. "You did a good job, Shea," he said, smiling at her. "The punishment is over. Just one last thing."

He reached for the clover clamps, gripping them with his index fingers and thumbs. Better just to do it quickly. He pressed the clamps to release the springs.

Predictably, Shea yelped with pain as the blood flow returned to her tortured nipples, her hands bunching into fists about her cuffs.

Impulsively, unable to resist, Zach lowered his head and suckled first one and then the other nipple, stroking them with his tongue, his balls aching. He reached for her heavy, lush breasts with his hands, eager to cup and massage them. Only Steve's murmured, "Zach," recalled him to his senses.

Zach pulled back from the girl, who was watching him, her lips parted, her eyes soft.

He turned his focus to Steve, who had brought over the stepladder and was in the process of releasing Shea's wrists from her cuffs. Zach caught her arms as they fell, guiding them gently to her sides. The two of them helped her from the brick, each holding an upper arm as she stepped down to the floor. They guided her to the recovery couch.

Without being told, she lay on her stomach and buried her face against her folded arms. Her ass and the backs of her thighs were bright red from the paddling. Zach reached for the Arnica gel from the side table and squeezed a generous portion onto his fingers.

Shea jumped at his initial touch but then settled against the cushions with a long, deep sigh.

Steve had crouched beside Zach in front of the girl. They exchanged a long look. There was something in Steve's expression that Zach couldn't quite read. At the same time, something was niggling in the back of his mind, or, more accurately, deep in his gut. *Danger*, it whispered. *Watch out, Zach. You have to keep your distance.* But Zach shook away the warning. He was having too much fun.

~*~

Shea sat on the couch between the two guys, a soft blanket wrapped around her shoulders, a mug of hot tea cradled in her hands. She hated that her behavior had resulted in a punishment, and the very idea of being punished had been humiliating. The paddling had hurt like hell, and her bottom was still sore. At the same time, she couldn't deny the deep, dark thrill she had experienced at being chained up, gagged and paddled, just like the sexy girls in the videos online.

The exercise had been amazing, once she'd managed to get past the fear of the unknown, once she'd stopped anticipating. Those texture gloves were so sensual, the leather so buttery soft, those wicked spikes scraping like tiny knives along her flesh.

And the orgasm! Oh, that orgasm was like nothing she'd ever experienced in her life. The orgasms she gave herself with her fingers and her toys had seemed satisfactory, but she realized now they were little more than scratching an itch. Whatever Master Zach had done with his fingers had been incredible.

But beyond that—being tied down as she'd been, with Sir Stephen looking down at her with those penetrating eyes…oh! Wouldn't it be wonderful to experience that again? Right now, in fact, would be a good time.

She shot a sidelong glance at each man and was disconcerted to find they were both regarding her, Master Zach's expression slightly quizzical, Sir Stephen's mildly amused.

Working to get herself under control, Shea took another sip of the cinnamon tea Master Zach had prepared using an electric kettle they kept on top of the mini refrigerator. If she couldn't have another orgasm, it would be nice to snuggle down between the two men and take a long, cozy nap. She wondered if napping was ever part of the session. Somehow she doubted it.

What was next? Would they allow her to finish her tea and then send her on her way?

A part of her wanted to go—to be alone to process the astonishing experience—but another part of her never wanted to leave.

"We need to talk, Shea," Sir Stephen said. So she was Shea now, no longer S. That made sense, she supposed, since the session was presumably over. But talk? Talk about what? The next session? Well, yes, that made sense.

"We do, Sir?" she said, just to say something.

"We do." He angled his body so he was facing her. "You mentioned you've never had an orgasm at the hands of another."

Shea felt the heat began to rise beneath her skin. "Oh, well," she said. "It was—I'm a, I mean..." She trailed off, uncertain what to say, how much to admit. If they knew how sexually inexperienced she actually was, would they both go running for the hills?

"It's nothing to be embarrassed about," Zach said from her other side. "A lot of women have a hard time climaxing, especially women like you who've only been with vanilla guys. People who are hardwired like we are need that little something extra."

"The right kind of erotic suffering and stimulation to take you where you need to go," Sir Stephen clarified.

"Yes!" Shea cried, looking from one guy to the other. "That's it exactly. That's what I've been missing."

"So, is Zach correct in assuming you've only been with vanilla guys?" Sir Stephen persisted.

Shea opened her mouth, the lie ready on her lips. All she had to do was say, "Yes, they've all been vanilla." But Master Zach's words from the initial interview came back to her— *"If you want to get anything out of this training, rigorous honesty is absolutely essential. Remember, we don't judge you."*

Praying that was true, she girded herself for her admission. After all, she would have to tell them sometime. They had the right to know. Her eyes down, she blew out a breath and then admitted, "I've never been with a man at all."

"I'm sorry, what?" Sir Stephen said.

Unable to look up, Shea repeated in a louder voice, "I've never been with a man at all."

Both men stiffened, and she could only imagine the looks they were exchanging over her head as she stared doggedly down into her mug, her face on fire. Was this when they kicked her out?

"You're a...virgin?" Master Zach said the word as if it were on par with *serial killer* or *child molester*.

Deeply embarrassed now, Shea retorted, "I suppose I'm not a virgin in the technical sense. I probably lost my hymen riding my bike when I was eight years old." She was aware of her icy tone but was somehow unable to stop herself. Maybe the ice would melt some of the heat in her face. "What's the big deal about virginity anyway? Why is it that vaginal intercourse is defined as the be-all and end-all? I don't even like the word *vagina*." She was babbling but was unable to stop. "Did you know that the word *vagina* is Latin for sheath or scabbard? How sexist is that? Defining the birth canal in relation to how it can serve the penis of a man. And just because—"

Sir Stephen placed two fingers over Shea's lips, startling her into silence.

"Shea, stop. Calm down. It's okay. There is absolutely nothing wrong with the fact that you're a virgin. We're just surprised, is all. You seem so sexually aware, so in touch with your masochistic and erotic feelings that we just naturally assumed you'd been in a relationship."

"Oh," Shea said, barking a short, embarrassed laugh. "Don't even get me started on relationships. I watch all my girlfriends mooning over these guys, finally going out with them, getting embroiled in all their nonsense and dysfunction, and then breaking up. Or worse, they marry them anyway and then get divorced two years later." She shook her head. "I mean, what's the point? Who needs all that drama? Not me, I can tell you."

"I hear you on that one," Zach said. "And I agree. Who needs the drama? I'm perfectly happy without a girlfriend."

Shea glanced from Zach to Steve. Steve's lips were pressed into a thin line, his expression difficult to read. After a moment, he slowly shook his head, his lips lifting into a smile that didn't reach his eyes. In a quiet voice, he said, "How about you, Shea? Are you happy being alone?"

"Who, me?" Shea replied stupidly. "I'm *totally* happy." Then, to her shocked dismay, she burst into tears.

CHAPTER 6

Steve instinctively reached to comfort Shea, while Zach, on her other side, did the same. They found themselves staring at each other as Shea leaped to her feet. Whirling to face them, she wiped away her tears with one hand while clutching the blanket around her shoulders with the other.

She smiled a brittle smile through the tears and forced a laugh. "Ha, just ignore me. I do this sometimes." She sniffed loudly. "It doesn't mean anything." She clutched the blanket tighter. "I should just go now. Yes, I need to go. It's late and—"

"And we haven't had our post-session coffee and pie," Zach interrupted as he rose from the couch.

Startled, Shea echoed, "Pie?"

Steve, who had been about to launch into a lecture about processing feelings, closed his mouth and flashed a grateful smile at his friend. Zach had a wonderful way of cutting to the heart of the matter without making people feel stupid or shutting them down. And he was right—no way could they let her go like this.

"There's a great little place not five minutes from here," Steve said, continuing the thread as he got to his feet. "Mama Mae's House of Pies."

"They have forty different kinds of pie," Zach said enthusiastically. "Each one better than the last."

"And he should know," Steve added with a laugh. "He's had every single one of them."

Shea was staring at them, the tears no longer falling. Steve put his arm around her shoulders. "Seriously, Shea, let's go get a cup of coffee and talk a little more before we call it a night, okay? You handled a whole lot during this session. Part of the process is talking things through afterward."

She opened her mouth as if to protest, but, as he stared into her unusual, gold-rimmed blue eyes, she seemed to reconsider. With a small nod, she said, "Okay. Pie and coffee."

Zach handed Shea her pile of clothing. "There's a bathroom just outside the dungeon, right by the washer and dryer. Get dressed, wash up, whatever you need to do. We'll wait for you upstairs, okay?"

The three of them drove together in Steve's car to Mama Mae's. Though it was after ten, the place was crowded, as always. They found an empty table near the back and took their seats. The table was already set with silverware, glasses and coffee mugs. Four large, laminated menus stood erect in a metal holder on the center of the table.

A plump, middle-aged waitress appeared a moment later, pad and pencil in her hand. "Evening," she said. She wore a white uniform and wedged white shoes, looking more like a nurse than a waitress. "Can I get you all something to drink?"

"Coffee," Zach said. "And water, too, please."

The waitress nodded brusquely and moved away.

Shea reached for a menu, which was covered in bright photographs of various pies alongside the lengthy list of selections. "Wow," she said as she scanned the pages. "You weren't kidding." She eyed the menu carefully. "I wonder if they cook the crust correctly on the coconut custard," she mused. "I hate it when it's soggy underneath."

"They cook it to perfection," Zach said, as Steve had known he would. "Light, flaky, the perfect vehicle for the custard."

Shea flashed a sweet, dimpled smile. "That's what I want then. Coconut custard pie."

The waitress appeared with two carafes—one of ice water and one of coffee—and set them directly on the table. She took their orders— the coconut custard for Shea, blueberry for Steve and apple with a scoop of vanilla ice cream on top for Zach.

Once she had gone, Zach poured them each a cup of coffee from the carafe. As they added sugar and cream, Steve said, "Let's talk a little about what happened back in the dungeon. Most people don't follow the statement, 'I'm totally happy' by bursting into tears. Can you tell us what that was about?"

"Oh." Shea waved a hand dismissively. "I told you—sometimes I'm just a little emotional. It doesn't mean anything. Please"—she fixed him with a suddenly pleading gaze—"can't we just let it go at that?"

Clearly there was more to the story, but Steve decided not to push it. "For now," he said aloud.

The waitress appeared with their plates, which she set in front of them. When she had gone again, and after taking a huge bite of his pie and following it with a big slurp of coffee, Zach said, "So, Steve and I were talking a little while you were getting dressed. We definitely want to keep going with your training. We're thinking at least three sessions a week, if that works for you."

"Yes," Shea said at once. "That's great. Absolutely." She smiled shyly, her eyes sparkling.

Steve had to squelch a crazy desire to take her into his arms. "You haven't touched your pie," he said, as much to distract himself as anything.

She looked down at her plate, as if surprised to find it there in front of her. She lifted her fork and took a bite, her eyes fluttering shut as she chewed. "Mmmm," she moaned appreciatively. Swallowing, she opened her eyes and focused on Zach, adding, "Perfect. Just like you said."

"Told you," Zach, who had nearly finished his, said with satisfaction.

"While you're not with us," Steve said, returning the focus to her training, "we'll give you a series of assignments and a set of rules you must observe if you're serious about your training."

"Okay," Shea said, her eyes fixed on his face.

"First rule," Steve continued, "is that you are never, ever, to touch yourself sexually without our express direction and permission."

Shea frowned. "Never?"

"That's right. Your body and your orgasms now belong to us."

Her frown melted away, her face softening with what Steve recognized as a submissive glow. How had this girl gone twenty-eight years without exploring her true nature? And what really lay behind those sudden tears?

"We'll send you an email each morning," Zach added as Steve took a bite of his pie, "with your specific assignments for the day. You'll report to us at the end of each day via email as to how it went. We'll want to know about your feelings and reactions—what you liked about the assignment, what you didn't like, how it made you feel—things like that. The information you provide will help us tailor your training as we move forward."

"Yes, Master Zach," Shea said softly, and for an odd moment Steve found himself wishing he was alone with Shea and that she had eyes only for him.

Shaking away the irrational feeling, he focused instead on expectations and goals going forward, as well as practical matters like Shea's email address and work schedule.

Zach ordered a second piece of pie—pecan this time—and after he'd wolfed it down, they left money on top of the bill and headed out into the parking lot.

As Steve drove them back to the house, Zach, who sat in the back with Shea, handed her the training duffel they'd put together for her while she was changing. "You'll find various items in the bag that will aid in your training," Zach explained. "Feel free to examine them, but don't use any of them until we give you explicit direction."

Steve glanced in the rearview mirror as Shea accepted the tote, a dubious expression on her face. "Yes, Sir," she said quietly.

Steve pulled his Audi into the garage and the three of them climbed out. They walked Shea to her car, an old Ford Taurus. Zach opened her car door for her, and she slipped into the driver's seat, setting the canvas bag on the seat beside her.

She started her engine, but before backing down the driveway, she rolled down her window and said, "Thanks for the pie and for"—she paused, a pink flush moving over her cheeks—"for everything."

~*~

As soon as she got home, Shea rushed into her bedroom. Pushing aside the discarded outfits from earlier that evening, she dumped the contents of the small duffel bag onto her bed. Inside she found a slim, black butt plug in its original shrink-wrap, along with a pair of alligator nipple clamps, a tube of lubricant, a ruler, a pair of black leather wrist cuffs with clips attached and a purple butterfly contraption with elastic straps and a remote control, the words *Wireless Venus Butterfly Erotic Novelty* written in large letters on the outside of the packaging.

Though she was exhausted—not only physically but mentally—from the extraordinary evening, she hurried to the kitchen and rummaged through the junk drawer to find a pair of scissors. Returning to the bedroom, she cut away the wrapping on the various toys. She was especially fascinated by the butterfly, which whirred appealingly against her palm as she turned on the small bullet-shaped remote control that came with it. She very nearly disregarded her trainers' mandate not to use any of the toys until directed by them—after all, who would know?

You would know.

Placing the items in the pouches that came with them and stowing them in the duffel, she went into the bathroom to get ready for bed. She hadn't thought she would sleep that night, her mind still teeming with details of the session, her body still tingling from the powerful orgasm, but the next thing she knew, her phone alarm was chiming beside her, the sun rising over the windowsill.

After turning off the alarm, she went at once to her email account, a jolt of excitement hurtling through her as she saw the message from *Hartman-Wilder-Trainers*. The message was short, and she instantly memorized its contents:

Good morning, S

Before you leave for work, insert the butt plug into your ass. You will leave the plug in place until your lunchtime, when you will go into the bathroom and remove it. You will masturbate at that time, but you are not to orgasm. Instead, when you are nearing orgasm, you will strike your vulva with your ruler until the urge to climax subsides. You will repeat this exercise of stimulating yourself nearly to orgasm and then hitting your cunt with the ruler two more times. You will not come during this exercise.

Later that morning as Shea stirred cream into her coffee mug at the break room counter, Harold, one of the other chemists in her lab, said, "Hey there, Shea. Sit down and try a piece of my wife's strudel. She made enough for an army and then didn't want it lying around the house."

Shea opened her mouth to automatically refuse—she never joined the others for their coffee break, usually too focused on whatever she was working on to take the time. But as she turned to see the group of guys—Harold, Denny, Aaron and even the ever-annoying Jeff—she found herself smiling. "Okay, sure. Thanks."

As she slid into the offered chair, she adjusted herself carefully to accommodate the slim butt plug she'd finally managed to insert that morning, using nearly half the tube of lubricant in the process.

To her surprise, save for a moment at the end of the insertion where the base of the plug flared a little, it hadn't hurt. She had been thrilled with herself for her accomplishment and had wanted to tell someone about it—but who? All her girlfriends were as vanilla as the blandest instant pudding, and they would be horrified if they knew what she was up to.

Then she had remembered her trainers' instruction to record her feelings in an email. Opening the email app on her phone, she had quickly typed her experience and feelings, not trying to censor any of it, but just letting it flow. Somehow, that had helped her to move on with her morning, and she'd dressed, eaten her cereal and headed out to work, with no one the wiser as to what was hidden inside her, or the wild fantasies playing out in her head.

As she had struggled to concentrate on her work that morning, she had shifted repeatedly on her stool in order to feel the plug lodged deep in her rectum, and she had had to press her thighs together in an effort to ease the constant throb of lust between her legs.

In spite of the erotic discomfort, or perhaps partially because of it, she felt incredibly alive—her awareness of everything around her heightened, as if the focus knob on her view of the world had suddenly been sharpened.

Sitting now at the table with her colleagues, she tried to follow the various threads of conversation taking place—Denny's new baby, Jeff's complaints about the secretarial pool, Harold's detailed description of the movie he and his wife had seen the previous weekend. She smiled and nodded, appropriately cooing over Denny's baby photos on his cell phone and even commiserating with Jeff on turnaround time.

"Something's different about you," Aaron said, staring at her intently. "Did you change your hair or something? Are you wearing makeup? You seem, I don't know"—he shrugged, still eying her intently—"all sparkly or something."

Shea, who still wore her hair clipped back at the nape of her neck to keep it out of her experiments and was wearing the same minimal makeup as always, felt the heat rise in her face, but she just shook her head with a smile. "I'm still the same old me," she lied.

Jeannie, Mr. Carroll's secretary, had entered the break room at the start of this interchange and now turned from the refrigerator where she was retrieving her snack. "Come on, guys, it's obvious. Shea's in love. It's written all over her face."

Before Shea could deny the ridiculous assertion, Jeff burst into obnoxious laughter, braying like a donkey. "Shea O'Connor in love? She doesn't even date, for Christ's sake. Underneath that lab coat, she wears a nun's habit."

Shea didn't rise to the bait, instead freezing Jeff mid-bray with an icy stare.

Turning to Jeannie, she smiled. "Actually, I am seeing someone," she said.

Two someones, to be precise.

After all, Aaron had noticed she was "sparkly" so why try to hide it? None of them needed to know the someones were trainers, or that she was only a client.

"Good for you," Jeannie said approvingly as she left the room.

"Now, if you gentlemen will excuse me," Shea said, pushing back from the table. "I'm taking an early lunch."

~*~

Zach sat on the dungeon couch beside Steve, their new trainee naked on the kneeling pad in front of them. He would have actually liked to take Shea with him to Hardcore and put her through her paces in public, but when he'd mentioned his thought to Steve, his partner had said, "Not yet, Zach. We don't want to push her too fast. She's already handling a lot for such a novice. Maybe we can take her next Saturday, depending on her progress over the course of the week."

Zach had been startled by Steve's use of the word "we" and it made him realize he hadn't been thinking about Steve as part of the equation when he had considered taking Shea out.

The thought pulled him up short. They had an unspoken but definite rule—neither of them dated one of their trainees until the training was officially over. It got too complicated otherwise, especially for Steve, who tended to get more emotionally involved than Zach.

It was kind of ironic, when he thought about it—Zach knew he came across as the lovey-dovey one—the more sensitive, gentle of the two, while Steve, who was more of a hardcore sadist than Zach, gave the impression he was also the more aloof, demanding Master. And Zach couldn't deny the combination of the two of them was an effective one. There was never a shortage of women eager to train with them. He sometimes joked with Steve that together they made the perfect Dom.

But in fact, beneath the rules, protocol and whips, Steve was the mush, his heart too easily broken, his defenses too easily penetrated, while Zach kept his emotions firmly out of the mix. He liked playing the field, and part of the fun was avoiding the potential landmines of emotional entanglement along the way. No way was he going to settle for one girl when there were so many lovely ladies just waiting to be trained, claimed, conquered and then sent, always with a tender kiss and swat on their ass, of course, on their merry way.

Shea was different, though, from anyone they had trained before. She was so disarmingly...genuine. Yes, that was the word. There was no hidden agenda, no sly topping from the bottom, no false moves. And though it shouldn't really matter for training purposes, there was the unusual yet intriguing complication of her virginity. Zach hadn't been with a virgin since...wait, he'd *never* been with a virgin.

His first serious girlfriend in high school had been a year older than he, and quite a bit more experienced. She'd been wet and ready and, though he'd only lasted about three minutes, he still remembered the first time he'd entered her velvety wet heat—the sudden grip of her vaginal muscles and her soft, yielding body beneath his. He'd heard plenty of horror stories from buddies about their wilting erections in the face of their girlfriend's nervous, anxious resistance, and he'd been more than glad to have dodged that particular bullet.

Returning his focus to the girl kneeling before them, Zach said, "We've been reading your emails, of course, and they've been very enlightening. We're looking forward to watching your video with you. Tell us a little about the process—how it went for you, what you were feeling."

Shea's cheeks began to redden. Her capacity to blush was astonishing but also rather sweet. She looked down at the floor as if gathering herself. Finally, she swallowed and lifted her gaze, focusing first on Steve and then on Zach, who gave her a reassuring smile. "You had me make a video of myself masturbating while I shared out loud a secret sexual fantasy—one I hadn't told you yet."

She paused again for so long that Zach prompted, "Go on. Remember, there is no right and wrong here. It's a process."

She flashed him a grateful look and nodded. "I kind of zoned out while I was doing it—I mean, I just sort of let go. The fantasy I came up with, I really have no idea where it came from. I mean, it's not anything I ever even imagined before..." She trailed off again.

"That sounds like a good development, S," Steve said. "One of your training goals is to let go of your inhibitions. An essential component of submission is to give yourself, to share of yourself, without holding back. If you come up with hot new fantasies in the process"—he shrugged and grinned—"so much the better."

"Exactly," Zach concurred. "Before we watch the video, tell us about today's assignment."

"Today I wore the butterfly to work. It took me a while to figure out how to put the darn thing on." Shea flashed a sudden grin. "You told me I should have five orgasms over the course of the workday using the butterfly. I couldn't use it in the lab, of course, because it makes too much noise, not to mention, I have a bunch of guys sitting around me." She grinned sheepishly.

"So, how did you manage?" Zach asked, imagining Shea at her office or lab or whatever it was, surrounded by other science geeks in white coats who had no idea what she had on inside her panties.

"I took a lot of bathroom breaks," she said with a small laugh. "Luckily, my time is pretty much my own, as long as I get my work done.

I really like my butterfly," she added enthusiastically, her words followed by another spectacular blush.

"Good to hear," Steve said with dry amusement. "Now, the recording of your masturbation. Where is that?"

"I put it on a thumb drive, like you said, Sir. It's on top of my cell phone in the top cubby. It's not—I mean, you're not going to use it for anything, or show it to anyone, right?" she asked, worry coloring her tone.

"Absolutely not," Zach assured her. "Once we've watched it, you'll keep the thumb drive in your possession."

"Thank you, Master Zach. Um, if it's okay, could you just, you know, watch it later, when I'm not around? I don't really want to see it."

Zach flashed Steve an amused glance before replying, "No, that's not okay. You'll sit between us here on the couch, and we'll watch it together."

She swallowed visibly but, after a moment's hesitation, replied, "Yes, Sir."

Zach retrieved the laptop and the thumb drive while Shea seated herself next to Steve. Zach returned and sat on her other side, noticing, not for the first time, the warm, inviting scent of vanilla on her skin, along with the light floral scent of her shampoo. Her long hair was over her shoulders, the tips covering the tops of her breasts. Zach gathered the long, unruly tendrils into a ponytail and smoothed them back behind her so he had a better view of her full, round breasts and the perky nipples at their centers.

Then he placed the laptop on her bare thighs, the thumb drive already in the USB port. He touched a key to unlock the screen, and a still of Shea, naked on a bed, appeared in front of them, a play arrow superimposed over the image.

"Yuck," Shea muttered, turning her head aside.

"Shea," Steve said sharply. "Would you rather start tonight's session with a punishment?"

"No, Sir. I'm sorry, Sir," Shea said hurriedly. "It's just—"

"Enough. You will remain silent until asked a direct question."

Shea glanced beseechingly at Zach, but he only nodded, crossing his arms over his chest for emphasis.

Slowly, she turned back to face the screen.

Steve leaned over and touched a key, and the image came alive.

Shea had set up whatever recording device she was using so there was a full view of the mattress. She appeared in front of the camera, naked, her face reddening as she lay down in the center of the bed. She placed her feet flat on the mattress and let her knees fall open, immediately covering her cunt with her right hand. Her large breasts were soft mounds on her chest, her hair loose and wild on the pillow. She began to speak in a low, halting murmur.

Zach reached unobtrusively to the side of the laptop to increase the volume.

"I'm in a cage in the corner of a large dining room," the girl in the video began. "There are several men seated around the table. They've just finished a meal and they're drinking glasses of brandy. Master Zach and Sir Stephen are at either end of the table. Nobody is paying any attention to me.

"'When are we going to get to sample your new slave?' one of the men at the table asks.

"'How about now?' Sir Stephen says. He stands and moves to my cage. He turns the lock and pulls the door open. He puts his hand on my throat." The girl in the video gasped, a tremor moving through her body.

Zach, who had already observed her sensitivity to chokeholds, made a mental note to explore that further in their training.

"Sir Stephen pulls me out of the cage, his fingers clamped below my jaw like a vise." The girl in the video stopped speaking as she rubbed herself for several seconds, the sound of her breathing audible.

Zach stole a sidelong glance at Shea beside him. Her face was as red as a tomato but her nipples were fully erect, and he bet if he slid his hand between her legs to take her temperature, he would find that she was hot and wet.

"'Lie on the table in front of Master Brandon and spread your legs so he can see your cunt, S,' Sir Stephen commands me. I'm shy about doing this, but I don't dare disobey or he'll whip me and keep me in the cage all night, like he did the last time."

Zach flashed a glance at Steve over Shea's head. *The last time?* he mouthed with raised eyebrows. Steve answered with an amused shrug. Clearly, the girl had a very active imagination.

Zach experienced a rush of gratitude that Shea was so willing to give of herself to the two of them. There was something about D/s that seemed to skip past so many of the social conventions that kept people at arm's length. It was one of the things he loved most about the scene.

At the same time, it didn't escape his notice that the fantasy was focused around Sir Stephen, though at least Master Zach was at the table. That made sense, he supposed, since, so far during their training sessions, Steve had been the one who had given most of the direct commands to the girl.

That was often the way between them, though this was the first time Zach had thought much about it. This was the first time it seemed, for some reason, to matter.

As Shea continued to talk and masturbate on the video, she described various scenarios involving the different guys at the table, each of whom did things to her while the others looked on. As she talked, her voice took on an increasingly breathy, husky tone, her fingers busy between her legs all the while. One guy whipped her cunt with a single tail, then another stood over the table and choked her with his cock, while yet another dripped hot wax on her breasts.

Zach was impressed at the narrative as he glanced from the screen to Shea seated beside him on the couch. She was biting her lower lip, her eyes fever bright as she watched herself approach orgasm on the small screen.

"Then Master Zach steps in front of me."

Finally, Zach thought with an inward grin.

"He opens his leather fly to reveal his massive cock," the girl on the screen said, while the girl beside him groaned.

Delighted with the recognition of his "massive cock," Zach shot a triumphant look toward Steve, who grinned and shrugged.

"'It's time,' he says in his deep, sexy voice. "You've been a virgin too long. Now you belong to me.'"

Again Zach and Steve exchanged a glance as Shea continued, "He places the head of his shaft between my legs and enters me." The girl in the video gasped as if it were really happening to her. "It hurts, but I welcome the pain. I *need* the pain. I need to suffer. I need to suffer for my Masters. I need—oh god, oh, oh, oooooh…"

Shea lifted her hips from the bed, a shudder wracking her body as she clamped her knees together and then fell back against the mattress with a cry. Her hand fluttered away from her cunt and she lay still for a long moment on the bed, the only sound her heavy breathing.

Finally, she lifted herself on her elbows and looked directly at the screen. "I can't believe I just did that," she muttered as she rocked herself forward. She reached toward the device, ending the video.

The living girl between them brought her hands to her face. "Oh, god, Sirs," she wailed. "I'm so embarrassed that you watched that."

Zach and Steve both reached for her hands, each pulling one away from her face.

Her wrist still caught in his grasp, Steve demanded, "Did you forget one of the primary rules of D/s? Modesty has no place in submission. You executed the assignment you were given, and you did it very well. But this little display of yours definitely calls for another correction."

"But first," Zach interjected, his cock throbbing, "I really think we need to address this issue of your virginity. It's obvious from what you've said when we've talked, as well as the action in your fantasy, that you're ready to be deflowered." He felt a little ridiculous saying the silly word, but didn't know how else to put it. "One of us will be happy to take care of that for you before we move on with your training."

Of course, based on her fantasy, he, Zach, would obviously be her chosen one.

Steve shot him a sharp look. They had in fact discussed the interesting fact of her virginity, but had agreed they would wait for her to broach the subject again.

Zach avoided meeting Steve's eye. Maybe she hadn't brought it up directly, but that fantasy was clearly a call for help, and he was just the man to provide such assistance. After twenty-nine years of avoiding virgins at all costs, he found himself quite ready to take the plunge.

To his surprise, Steve agreed. "I think that's a good idea, Shea. Zach's right. Your virginity might be something of a roadblock as we get deeper into training. Let's address it and move on. Which one of us would you like to have fuck you?"

Shea stared from one to the other of them, her face actually draining of color for a change. Zach was afraid she was going to faint, but just as he reached out to steady her, Shea said, "Both of you, please, Sirs."

CHAPTER 7

"I think we'll be more comfortable upstairs for this particular, uh, exercise. You agree, Zach?"

Zach glanced at Shea and then regarded Steve for a long moment before finally nodding. "Yeah, that makes sense."

It had been fascinating to watch Shea on the screen, alone in her bedroom, her hand between her legs, as she painted such a vivid scenario with her words. Her voice had been husky with lust, her gasps pulled from deep inside. It had been more than just a window to her secret fantasies. Steve had gotten a sense of the real woman behind the somewhat shy, occasionally awkward new trainee. Virgin or not, Shea was clearly very in touch with her submissive and masochistic feelings, and extremely sexually responsive.

They led her out of the dungeon and up the stairs to the first floor. "Let's go up to my bedroom," Steve said. "The bed is bigger." *And it's mine, not Zach's. Did that matter? No,* Steve told himself firmly. *Zach and I are a team.*

On the second floor, they walked down the hallway past Zach's room and the guest bedroom to the large master bedroom, Shea naked between them. Steve stopped at the door and gestured for the pair to enter ahead of him.

Shea stepped into the room, stopping abruptly as she took in Steve's king-size bed on its high wooden frame and the three decorative whips he'd hung above the headboard.

Zach neatly sidestepped the immobile girl and entered the room. Turning to Shea, who had wrapped her arms protectively around her bare breasts, he said, "So, you sure about both of us? I mean, you can only lose your virginity"—he used his fingers to put quotations around the phrase—"once, right?"

"Actually, that's not true," Steve interjected, his balls already tight with anticipation, his heart beating just a little too fast. They both turned their heads toward him. "Zach will take you vaginally," he managed to say evenly, "and I'll take you anally."

Shea's mouth opened, her eyes widening as she took a step back, her arms still wrapped tightly around her body.

"S," Steve said with quiet authority, consciously using only her initial to help her return to the proper mindset, "drop your hands to your sides and stand at attention, feet shoulder-width apart, back straight."

He waited until she had complied, pleased to see some of her submissive calm returning in the process. "Do you have an issue with anal sex?"

Shea swallowed visibly, a play of emotions moving over her face that included both fear and desire. He waited, his gaze fixed on her face. Finally, she said, "No, Sir Stephen."

Satisfied, Steve moved to the bed and pulled down the covers. "Lie on your back right here," he said, pointing to the side of the bed he didn't sleep on. Shea obeyed him, settling herself against the sheets. Turning to Zach, he said, "Vaginal first?"

"Works for me." Zach flashed a broad grin, not even trying to hide his obvious eagerness.

Zach stripped quickly. His cock fisted in his hand, he turned to Steve. "Condoms?"

Steve reached into the drawer of his nightstand and tossed a packet, along with a tube of lubricant, to Zach, who caught the items easily, tore open the wrapper and slid the pre-lubricated sheath over his large, erect shaft. Then he sat on the edge of the bed beside Shea and placed his hand on her right breast. "This is a new step forward for you."

"It's no big deal," Shea asserted with a defiant lift of her chin "I really don't understand what all the drama is about."

Her body language belied her words, her nipples erect, her voice wavering slightly, the same fever-bright look in her eyes he'd seen in the video. Steve looked forward to showing her precisely what all the drama was about.

He glanced at Zach to see his reaction to Shea's claim. Zach grinned and said in typical Zach fashion, "You don't need drama to have fun, babe. It's about time you learned just what it is you've been missing."

Whatever happened, every experience with Shea so far had been more intense than the last. They were still calling her their trainee, but they were about to move into uncharted waters, blurring the lines between trainee and lover in a way they'd never done before.

Crouching between her spread legs, Zach squeezed some lube onto his fingers and leaned forward to gently rub Shea's cunt in slow, easy circles. "Just relax," he said softly.

Shea moaned softly as Zach stroked her. When he inserted a finger inside her, she gasped. The girl was ready, ripe for the plucking.

Though he had never minded sharing with Zach when they played with girls at the club, for a moment, Steve experienced a small spasm of jealousy—he wanted to be the one to claim Shea in all ways.

No. As much as Steve hated to admit it, Zach was especially adept at staying in tune with a woman's body, and was therefore the best one to go first. Based on Shea's reaction to her first "deflowering," they would decide if she could handle more.

Steve unzipped his fly and let his cock loose from its confines as he moved to stand just beside Shea's head on the bed. The bouquet of her sexual arousal mingled with the soft vanilla scent of her perfume. Steve stroked himself as he watched Zach prime the girl, biding his time.

When she began to pant, her hips lifting in response to Zach's touch, Zach let his hand fall away and hoisted himself over her.

Shea made a nervous, mewling sound in her throat, her legs clamping shut as her hands rose to grab Zach's arms, as if to stop him from going any further.

"Arms at your sides, S," Steve ordered. "Offer yourself to Master Zach. Show your grace."

Shea released her grip on Zach's forearms, her hands falling to her sides as she turned to Steve. "Yes, Sir," she said in a tremulous voice.

Zach stroked her face tenderly. "You know you need this," he said. "You know you want it."

"Yes," she murmured, her legs falling open, her body relaxing. "Yes, Master Zach."

Zach guided his cock between her legs, his face a study in careful concentration. Steve's cock tingled with sympathetic longing.

"Ouch!" Shea cried, forgetting all about any submissive grace as she jerked beneath him.

Zach glanced at Steve. "You want to distract her a little?" He gave a nod toward Steve's erection.

"Absolutely," Steve agreed readily, that having been his plan all along. Moving closer to the bed, he leaned over and grabbed a handful of Shea's hair. "Have you ever sucked cock before?" he asked, his shaft hovering inches from her face.

"No, Sir Stephen," Shea gasped, her eyes fixed on his erection, her tongue suddenly visible on her upper lip. How had this sensual woman made it twenty-eight years without any sexual experience?

"We'll teach you proper technique in the dungeon. For now," he said as he placed the head of his cock between her parted lips, "I'm going to fuck your face while Zach fucks your cunt. Your only job is to keep your mouth open and your teeth off my cock. Use your lips and your tongue, and take what I give you."

Her eyes fixed on his cock, Shea nodded. "Yes, Sir Stephen."

His fingers still tangled in her hair, he pushed his cock a few inches past her lips. He groaned with pleasure as he entered her warm, soft mouth. He was back in his Dominant zone—his comfort zone—and it felt good. He forced himself to resist the impulse to glide his shaft all the way down her throat in one smooth thrust and hold it there until she surrendered completely.

Zach, meanwhile, had returned to his task, his hips moving slowly and gently over the girl trapped beneath him. She gave a muffled yelp against Steve's cock at what Steve presumed was the moment of penetration, and a deep shudder moved through her body.

"That's it," Zach encouraged. "You did it."

Shea's legs circled Zach's back, her hands reaching for his broad shoulders. She was no longer resisting. She was fully engaged in the erotic dance.

Steve could have stepped back then, but he kept his grip on her hair, forcing her head to the side as he slid his cock in and out of her mouth. Each time he thrust, he pushed a little farther back toward her throat. Shea gurgled and moaned against Steve's shaft, taking everything he gave her, while Zach lifted and lowered himself over the girl, his hips swiveling between her legs.

It wasn't long before a coiling sensation in Steve's balls announced imminent ejaculation. He didn't want to come though, not yet, not like this. He released his grip on her hair and stepped slowly back until his cock slid from her parted lips.

Shea's eyes opened, and she fixed a wide-eyed, anxious gaze on his face. "Is something wrong, Sir?" she gasped. "Am I bad at this? Did I hurt you?"

Steve smiled as he bent down to stroke her hair. "No, S. You did good. Now I want you to focus on what's happening. Give yourself over to Master Zach. Let him take you where you need to go."

Relief flooded her face, and she nodded. "Yes, Sir Stephen," she whispered.

Steve took a step back. As Shea's eyes fluttered shut once more, he began to quietly strip off his clothing, ready and aching to claim her.

Shea moaned as Zach continued to fuck her, the sound low and sensual in the back of her throat. Her arms were wrapped around Zach's broad back, her fingers digging into his flesh. All at once, she cried out, "Oh my god! What's happening? Oh, oh, oh…"

Lifting himself, Zach reached for Shea's arms and extended them over her head, pressing them by the wrists into the mattress. Then he resumed pummeling the girl, his pelvis pumping like a piston as she held tight with her legs around his back.

Her moan began to rise up a musical scale until she was mewling like a little kitten, her entire body trembling beneath Zach's. All at once, Zach stiffened and groaned, the sound a deep counterpoint to Shea's keening cries.

Zach collapsed against the girl, and they lay like that for several long moments, until, impatient for his turn, Steve tapped Zach's shoulder. With a grunt, Zach rolled away from Shea and onto his back beside her.

Shea lay completely limp, her knees splayed apart, the petals of her labia engorged and shiny with lubricant, her nipples dark pink marbles in the center of those large, perfect breasts.

As Steve stared down at her, his cock throbbing, Shea opened her eyes. As she focused on him, a beatific smile lifted the corners of her mouth and traveled up into her eyes. "Oh, my," she breathed, looking from Steve to Zach. "So *that's* what all the fuss was about."

~*~

Okay, Shea told her scientific self, *so you disproved the hypothesis that sex is overrated. Admit it—your hypothesis has been blown out of the water. Having a big, sexy hunk of a man on top of you, his huge cock moving inside you is not the same as using a dildo. No comparison. None.*

Even as she silently engaged in this discourse with herself, Shea's spirits were humming, singing, laughing and dancing. Though her pussy was sore—she'd felt the skin tear at her perineum at the initial moment of penetration—the lingering pleasure of her unexpected orgasm continued to suffuse her being. It had been different from any other climax she had experienced, either at her own hand or at the hand of her trainers. It was softer, more like a rolling, encompassing swell, rather than the crashing, resounding wave of direct clitoral stimulation, but no less powerful.

She wanted to do it again.

She glanced at Sir Stephen, who stood completely naked beside the bed, his beautiful, erect cock cradled in his hand—the cock she had sucked only moments before. She imagined Sir Stephen suddenly on top of her, his hand on her throat as he stroked her from the inside out with his cock. Would it be un-submissive of her to ask that he, too, take his place on top of her? She wanted to find out if it would feel different with another man.

Just as she opened her mouth to form the words, Sir Stephen said, "Recovery time is over. Get on your hands and knees, S. Offer yourself to me."

Shea's mouth snapped shut, her mind going suddenly blank with anxiety as she stared up at him without moving.

Sir Stephen took a step closer, his expression hardening.

Shea glanced at Master Zach, who had lifted himself to a sitting position beside her on the bed. He had removed the used condom and cleaned himself with a washcloth. He was still naked, his cock now at half-mast. "Go on," he said quietly. "Do as you're told."

Aware she was being disobedient, Shea forced herself to obey the two men. Rolling from her back to her stomach, she positioned herself on her hands and knees on the mattress.

"Lower your forehead to the mattress," Sir Stephen directed. "You can cradle your head in your arms if that's more comfortable."

As Shea dropped her head down, Sir Stephen addressed Master Zach. "Why don't you sit in front of Shea at the head of the bed? You can help her with position and focus."

Master Zach shifted himself on the bed until he was in front of Shea. He extended his long, muscular legs on either side of her shoulders.

Sir Stephen, meanwhile, positioned himself behind her on the bed. "Your job, S," he said, "is to take what you're given without resistance.

Just like when you use the anal plug, the more you can relax, the easier it will be for you."

Shea startled when the cold goo of lubricant smeared against her asshole. Sir Stephen circled the rim with his fingertip. "Relax your body, Shea," he directed. "Remember, submission is giving of yourself. I don't want you to resist me. I want you to internalize what I'm saying, and obey, just as you've been doing in the dungeon."

He eased one finger inside her, the unexpected, sudden penetration pulling a startled cry from her lips, though it hadn't hurt at all. Actually, it felt kind of good as he moved his finger in a slow, easy circle inside her.

As he inserted a second finger, the sudden increased pressure caused her to tense against him.

"Relax," Sir Stephen reminded her, though his tone was gentle rather than reproving.

At the same time, Master Zach reached beneath her and lightly slapped her breasts, his hard palms stinging pleasantly over her flesh.

As Sir Stephen pushed yet another finger inside her, Shea yelped.

Master Zach gripped her nipples, giving them a sharp twist that made her forget, for a moment at least, what was happening behind her.

Sir Stephen's fingers were withdrawn, and Shea could feel him shifting on the mattress. Instinctively, she glanced back to see what he was doing. He was in the process of rolling a condom over his shaft. "Eyes straight ahead," he snapped and Shea faced quickly forward. Her heart was hammering in her chest, her body tensed once more in anticipation.

"Stop resisting," Master Zach admonished gently. "Remember, you want this. You need this."

It was on the tip of Shea's tongue to refute this. She had not asked for anal penetration—that had been Sir Stephen's idea. Yet she couldn't deny that, while afraid, she was thrilled to be on her hands and knees between these two sexy guys. And yes, though she hadn't known it until he said it, she did want this, too. She did need it.

"Yes, Sir," she said, flashing a grateful smile to the man who had shown her in glorious, fabulous detail, just what all the drama was about.

"I'm going to fuck your ass now," Sir Stephen announced from behind her. "I want you to reach back and offer yourself to me. Spread your ass cheeks and hold them open while I penetrate you."

Scorching heat moved over Shea's face and throat at the thought of exposing herself in that way—at the thought of him staring down at her puckered hole. *Get over it* she silently admonished herself. *It's nothing these guys haven't seen before.*

Reaching back, and using her forehead for balance against the mattress, Shea placed her hands on either side of her ass and pulled her cheeks apart. She drew in a sharp breath when the head of Sir Stephen's cock nudged at her nether hole. As he began to push his way inside her, Master Zach reached beneath her body and cupped her breasts in his large hands.

In spite of the welcome distraction of his touch, Shea's focus was wrenched back to her ass as Sir Stephen penetrated her. She jerked at the sudden, sharp pain, and might've twisted completely away from him, but Sir Stephen stopped her, his hands digging into her hips as he held her in place.

"Offer yourself," he admonished. "Give yourself to me."

The pain had lessened, and Shea could feel that her sphincter muscles were loosening, in spite of her fear. She could do this. She *was* doing it.

"Push back slowly against me," Sir Stephen commanded. "Impale yourself on my shaft, S. Take me inside."

Master Zach pressed gently against her shoulders in encouragement, and Shea slowly forced herself back, pushing past her own trembling resistance as she took Sir Stephen's cock deeper inside her ass.

"Yes," Sir Stephen breathed behind her. "That's it, S. You belong to me now."

His words reverberated deep in Shea's core. *You belong to me now.*

He began to move inside her, easing out and then pressing in, holding her in place, his hands on her hips. The pain melted away as he moved inside her, his swiveling thrusts sending spirals of hot, buttery pleasure through her core.

All at once, his right hand fell away and he smacked her ass with a resounding, startling sting that would have sent her sprawling forward had he not held her in place with his left hand. He smacked her again, thrusting hard inside her as he did so.

The pain exploded against the pleasure in perfect balance. For several long, delicious minutes he continued to spank and fuck her. But, as his hand continued to crash relentlessly against her, the pain began to overtake the pleasure.

"Ow, ow, ow," she heard someone chanting. It took her a second to realize it was she.

In response, Sir Stephen only hit her harder, thrusting deeper as he blistered her ass with his hard palm.

Shea began to pant, trying to process the pain as the tears sprang to her eyes. Panic started to rise in her gut. It was too much. She couldn't handle it.

I could say my safeword. I could make it stop.

No.

Master Zach leaned forward, extending his arm beneath her. He began to stroke her clit with his fingers as Sir Stephen continued to strike her just as hard as before, his cock thrusting deep inside her. The pain and the pleasure began to wind around each other, twisting and braiding into something more intense, more powerful than either experience on its own.

Shea felt as if flames were licking her entire body, heating her from the inside out, like molten lava threatening to spill from the volcano of her lust. Every cell was firing, every nerve ending poised.

"Oh my god, oh my god, oh, oh, oh," somebody was moaning.

With the last vestige of her conscious mind, somehow Shea managed to croak, "Please, Sirs, please, may I come? Oh god, *please...*"

Over the pounding of her heart and the ragged pant of her breath, Shea thought she heard—prayed she heard, "Yes, S. You may come."

Shea was lying on her back on the bed. She breathed in the mingled scents of citrus, bay rum and male sweat. Slowly, she opened her eyes. Master Zach was stretched out on one side of her, Sir Stephen on the other. "Welcome back," Master Zach said as he lifted himself to one elbow and smiled at her.

Shea smiled dreamily back, speech having, for the moment, deserted her. She turned her head slowly to regard Sir Stephen on her other side.

"Hey," he said, a gentleness in his tone she had never heard before. "How does it feel to no longer be a virgin?"

How did it feel?

Shea started to shrug—to minimize her feelings, to draw the old, familiar protective cover of scientific analysis over her potential vulnerability. But she stopped herself.

Rigorous honesty.

"Different," she admitted. "New. Or, not new, exactly, but like I've finally let go of a false self, something I don't want anymore, something I no longer need." As she said the words, she realized just how very true they were. The speed of her own transformation astounded her.

There was more to what she was feeling—something new and dangerous—something she wasn't quite ready to admit yet, at least not to these two men who suddenly mattered to her in a way she hadn't expected or anticipated. Pushing these confusing feelings aside, she refocused on their question.

How did it feel?

She sat up abruptly, and looked from one guy to the other, not trying to hide her wonderment. "I think I've spent my whole life walking in my sleep. I feel, *finally*, awake, alert and alive." She wrapped her arms around herself and grinned, trying to put a name to the budding, bubbling feeling inside her, something new and fragile, but determined to express itself.

And then she had it—that elusive emotion so new, so unexpected, that it had taken her a while to give it a name.

"Happy," she said with a sudden, spontaneous laugh. "For the first time in my life, I think I might actually be happy."

CHAPTER 8

Zach came out to the front porch and handed Steve a beer. His own bottle in hand, he sat beside him. It had been an unusually warm July for Portland and, even though it was close to midnight, they were quite comfortable in the T-shirts and jeans they'd pulled on after the amazing session with Shea in Steve's bedroom.

Though they had planned in theory to actually do some dungeon training that evening after removing the "roadblock" of Shea's virginity, they'd all agreed she'd had more than enough to handle for one night.

And not only her.

Zach was still trying to figure out how he felt about what all had gone down. Though he and Steve had played together with girls before, it had always been in the context of club scenes. It had been casual, fun, unimportant.

"You okay?" Steve asked, turning to regard him.

"Yeah, I'm good. Kind of blown away, but good." Zach took a long pull on his beer. He was still stunned by how powerful the experience had been. While he loved to fuck, it had always been just a kind of extension of masturbation, if he was being brutally honest about it. His own hand, a girl's hand, her mouth, her cunt—it all led to the same thing in the end—an orgasm. His orgasm.

And while he enjoyed the power rush of making the woman climax in the process, he realized now it had always been about him. About his power, his ability, *his* accomplishment.

Yet with Shea, somehow it had been different. He'd wanted to make her first time something special, not as an extension of his ego, but because she'd honored him—honored the two of them—with the gift of her virginity just as much as she had with the gift of her submission. Her trust was so simple and so honest, and he'd been touched in a way no other woman had reached him before.

But there was even more to it. Shea had linked them together in a way that went beyond just two trainers working with the same sub. That was a linear experience, a straight line with a Dom on either end, the sub in the center. But tonight had been something different, more like a circle in which all three of them had moved, joined by the power of the shared experience, connected by an intimacy that was new for Zach.

"That *was* pretty fucking intense," Steve agreed. He took a swig of beer. "I guess we just take things one step at a time, and see where we go from here."

"Yeah," Zach replied. "We can call Shea in the morning, once she's had a night to sleep on it. Let's meet her for breakfast or something and see where she's at with all this. Could be she wants to keep things strictly professional and continue exclusively with dungeon training."

"That is something we have to consider. And if that's what she wants, we would have to respect her wishes," Steve said, his face difficult to read.

Zach's shoulders lifted in their customary shrug, but he stopped himself. Whatever had started up there in the bedroom, he didn't want to ruin it with his usual who-gives-a-shit-what-happens attitude. "Yeah," he agreed. "But I sure hope that's not the case. I want more with her, however that plays out between the three of us."

"Me, too," Steve agreed with a fervency that surprised Zach. "A lot more."

~*~

That Saturday morning Shea jogged along the streets of her neighborhood in her new running shoes, filled with a vibrant energy she needed to work off. She could still feel the slight tear at the entrance of her pussy from the initial penetration, but that only served to remind her of what had transpired the night before and, as such, she cherished the sting.

She used to run regularly, but had lost the habit somewhere along the way. It felt good to be outside, moving her body, the body that had been claimed by two amazing guys. The blissful feelings of the night before had followed her into sleep and had remained upon waking. Beneath them were wonder and confusion.

Having spent her entire adult life trying to avoid the drama of a relationship, she had suddenly dived headlong into…into what? She couldn't lie to herself anymore—whatever had happened last night between the three of them, it was more than just another training exercise. It was about way more than just losing her virginity. That was for damn sure.

Her cell phone vibrated on the sports band she wore around her arm, and she glanced at it, her heart doing a flip-flop when she saw who it was. Coming to an abrupt halt, she pulled her phone from the slot and read the message.

"Good morning, Shea. Zach and I hope you slept well. We were thinking it would be a good idea if we three got together to talk. Are you up for breakfast or lunch?"

Eagerly, Shea texted back. *"Sure. Either is fine. Nothing on my schedule today."*

"Okay," came back the rapid reply. *"How about let's meet for breakfast at ten? You pick the place and we'll meet you there."*

The guys were already sitting across from each other in the booth at the diner Shea had selected, glasses of orange juice and mugs of coffee in front of them. Shea slid into the booth next to Steve and said breathlessly, "Sorry I'm late. My stupid car wouldn't start again."

"That old Taurus?" Zach asked.

Shea nodded. "It's always acting up. I swear it's in the shop more than in my parking lot. I'll probably have to bite the bullet soon and buy a new car, but my lease is up soon, and they always raise the darn rent, so I want to wait and see how much of a hit that'll be."

Aware she was babbling, Shea was relieved when the waitress appeared with a carafe of coffee in her hand and gestured toward Shea's empty mug. As the waitress filled her cup, Shea picked up the menu to glance through it.

"You all ready to order?" the waitress asked.

"How about you, Shea?" Zach asked. "Do you need more time?"

"No," Shea said, closing the menu. "I'll have the fresh fruit platter." Shockingly, she wasn't forcing herself to "be good" in front of the guys. She genuinely didn't want the big, gooey carb fest of a huge stack of pancakes with a side of bacon that she would have normally ordered. Since she'd met Steve and Zach, her appetite seemed to have vanished. Or, not vanished, but changed. She was actually eating only when hungry, rather than for comfort or distraction. She walked past the cookie and ice cream aisles at the supermarket, opting instead for fish, fresh fruit and vegetables.

Zach had no such reservations, and he ordered two eggs over-easy plus blueberry pancakes with a side of ham. Steve asked for scrambled eggs and toast.

"So," Steve said, "other than the car, how are you this morning, Shea?"

"I'm good, thanks," she said, unable to stop the smile that leaped to her face as she looked from Steve to Zach. "Last night was *amazing*," she gushed before she could stop herself. Heat licked at her cheeks, and she looked down at her coffee, suddenly afraid she'd been over-forward.

Steve moved closer to her on the booth bench, while Zach reached across the table and placed his hand on hers. "It was pretty amazing for us, too, Shea," he said softly.

She lifted her gaze to meet his. He was smiling at her. "Steve and I have been talking it over, and we agree we want to expand your training to include sexual service. Last night made it pretty clear this isn't a typical trainers/trainee relationship."

Shea nodded, her pulse picking up speed.

Steve spoke. "We want to explore our relationship with you beyond sessions in the dungeon. But we get that you might not be comfortable with that. You know, 'the drama' of it all." He made quotation marks in the air with his index fingers.

In spite of herself, Shea laughed, some of her tension easing away. "I want more, too," she admitted. Drama or no, Shea had come too far to turn back now. What would her girlfriends think if they knew she was falling not just for two guys but two Masters? And even more astoundingly, they might be falling for her, too?

After breakfast, Shea followed the guys to their house, having eagerly agreed to an impromptu session. She was both nervous and excited to leap into the sexual service aspect of submission, though not one hundred percent certain what she had signed up for. She definitely wanted more of those astounding orgasms, but beyond that, she wanted to serve these two amazing men. She wanted to please them and make them proud.

Once inside, the guys led Shea down to the dungeon. Though still a little self-conscious, she obediently stripped at the door. She was intrigued when both the guys stripped as well, though they stopped before removing their underwear.

They directed Shea to a padded mat in the center of the dungeon and had her kneel, back straight, hands resting lightly on her thighs, her knees spread to indicate accessibility.

Master Zach wore white boxers that hugged his small ass and muscular thighs, while Sir Stephen sported black bikini briefs that accentuated the sexy bulge at his crotch. She couldn't decide which of the guys was hotter.

"For this session, we'll begin your training in oral sex," Sir Stephen said. "Am I correct in assuming that, apart from last night, you've never worshiped a man's cock?"

Until last night, Shea had never even *seen* a man's cock, except in videos and photographs, much less worshiped one. "Yes, Sir," she replied, her stomach fluttering.

"Master Zach has *generously* agreed to allow you to begin training on him, while I offer instruction." Sir Stephen and Master Zach flashed conspiratorial grins at one another. "Since you're so new to this, we'll start with the basics and work up from there. For now, just focus on getting used to the feel of a man's cock in your mouth."

Master Zach moved closer until he was standing directly in front of Shea, his crotch only inches from her face. Sir Stephen stood beside the two of them, close enough to reach down and touch Shea.

"First," Sir Stephen directed, "you must ask for permission to worship your Master's cock. You will begin by kneeling forward to kiss the tops of your Master's feet. Then you will kneel back into position and say, 'Please, Sir, may I worship your cock?'"

Shea hesitated. "Now, Sir?" she asked.

"Now," Sir Stephen affirmed.

Shifting on the mat, Shea leaned forward and lowered herself until her head was just above Master Zach's bare feet. Feeling at once a little ridiculous and a lot thrilled, she touched her lips to the tops of his feet, one at a time.

Kneeling back on the mat, she looked up at Master Zach and said, hoping she got the words right, "Please, Sir, may I worship your cock?"

"Yes," Master Zach replied. "You may."

Now what?

She looked to Sir Stephen, who said, "Your next task is to remove your Master's underwear. You will fold them neatly and place them on the floor beside him."

Taking a deep breath, Shea leaned forward and reached for the elastic waistband of Master Zach's boxers. She pulled them past his narrow hips and down his muscular legs, unable to stop the slight tremble in her fingers as she did so.

Even in a semi-erect state, his cock seemed huge to her. It was hard to believe she had accommodated that thing inside her. Was she really supposed to suck it? She glanced helplessly toward Sir Stephen.

"Now kiss the head of his cock," Sir Stephen instructed in a patient voice that calmed her a little. "Just a light, closed mouth kiss of respect, and then thank him for his permission."

Heart beating a mile a minute, Shea leaned close and touched the spongy crown of Master Zach's cock with her lips. The scent of his musk shot directly to her cunt, which ached with the muscle memory from the night before. She wanted him to fuck her again, then and there on the dungeon floor, and her pussy actually spasmed with need.

"Thank you, Sir," she managed in a hoarse voice. She cleared her throat.

"Now gently cradle his balls in your hands." As he spoke, Sir Stephen placed his hand lightly on Shea's shoulder. Shea couldn't help noticing his hard-on.

She reached tentatively for Master Zach's balls and cupped them lightly in her palms. They were warm and soft, like furry plums that shifted beneath his skin. As she touched him, his shaft stiffened and elongated, the head nudging her cheek.

Startled, she jerked back, his balls still caught in her hands.

Master Zach placed a firm hand on her head. "Hey, careful with the family jewels," he said. "No squeezing allowed."

"Oh!" Shea cried, embarrassed. "Sorry." She loosened her grip, her face burning.

"Let's try that again, shall we?" Sir Stephen said. "Eventually this ritual will become second nature to you. But for now, I'll continue to guide you through the process from the beginning. You will start by kissing your Master's feet as a signal that you wish to serve him in some way. Then you will ask if you may worship his cock. Once he gives permission, you will remove his underwear, fold it neatly and place it on the floor by his feet. Then you will kiss the head of his cock as a gesture of respect, and thank him verbally for his permission."

"Yes, Sir," Shea replied, rapidly reviewing his instructions in her head and praying that she got them right.

Master Zach, meanwhile, had pulled his boxers back into place, though his now fully erect penis strained at the fly.

Feeling slightly silly, Shea leaned down once more and kissed the tops of his feet. She asked for permission to worship his cock, and it was granted.

It was harder to get his boxers off this time, his huge cock catching in the confines of the fabric. Shea waited for Sir Stephen to rebuke her for her clumsiness, but to her relief, he said nothing as she managed to get the boxers down Master Zach's legs.

Then Shea leaned forward again and once more kissed the crown of Master Zach's shaft with her lips. "Thank you for permission, Sir."

"You're welcome, S."

It was the first time Master Zach had used her first initial instead of her name, and the usage had the effect of sending her directly to a calmer, more submissive headspace.

"Now cradle his balls, gently this time," Sir Stephen directed.

Shea cupped the heavy, delicate balls in her hands.

"Better," Sir Stephen said. "Now you may worship Master Zach's cock. Just the head for now."

Praying she didn't make a fool of herself, Shea stuck out her tongue and tentatively touched the surprisingly silky-soft flesh. She ran her tongue in a circle around it and then brought her lips experimentally over the tip of the massive cock, wondering how she'd ever take the whole thing into her mouth. As she licked across the top of his cock, she encountered something gooey. Startled, she pulled back and made a face, belatedly realizing what she'd tasted must be pre-come, which she knew from her reading acted as a lubricant during intercourse.

"Back in position, S," Sir Stephen snapped. "Nobody told you to stop."

"I'm sorry, Sir," Shea said, embarrassed.

"Apology accepted, but since you interrupted the rhythm of the process, you will begin again. You'll start by kissing the tops of your Master's feet and continue with the rest of the ritual. We'll keep at it until you get it right."

Shea bit back a frustrated retort that she didn't want to start over. She wasn't even sure she wanted to continue with this exercise. Master Zach's cock was obviously too big for her mouth. It was better suited for her pussy. She would have rather they returned to Sir Stephen's bedroom for a repeat performance of the night before.

Yet, if she were honest, beneath her impatience and frustration, she truly wanted to please her Masters. She would try again, and hopefully this time she would do better.

She finally managed to get through the initial steps of the exercise without any hitches. She began to lick and suckle the head of Master Zach's cock while gently cradling his soft, heavy balls.

Sir Stephen tapped her shoulder. "That's good," he said. "Now move your head slowly forward, taking more of the shaft into your mouth. Your ultimate goal is to take the entire length of your Master's cock into your throat."

I'll never be able to do that, Shea thought, but she opened her mouth wider as she brought her head slowly forward over Master Zach's thick shaft.

It filled her mouth, pressing on her tongue so that she gagged reflexively. Startled, she pulled her head back, her hands falling away from his balls. For one horrible moment, she feared Sir Stephen would make her start the ritual again from the beginning.

To her relief, he only placed his hand gently on the back of her head. "Place your hands behind your back so you can focus better on Master Zach's cock." Sir Stephen waited a moment as Shea complied, and then continued, "This is as much a mental exercise as it is physical, S. It's about accepting what is given to you by your Master, even when to do so is hard for you. Now, take your time as you move forward. Open your throat and give yourself a chance to adjust."

Grateful for their patience, Shea tried again. She took a few inches of Master Zach's cock into her mouth and closed her lips gently around it. She could feel the pulse of his vein against her tongue. This wasn't so bad. In fact, it was pretty damn sexy to be naked and on her knees with a gorgeous man's cock in her mouth. She could do this!

Encouraged, she took more of the shaft into her mouth. She resisted the urge to gag, consciously trying to open her throat, though she didn't really know what that meant. She stroked the underside of Master Zach's cock with her tongue as she slid her lips up and down the top half of his cock.

Master Zach groaned quietly and thrust forward, just a little. But it was enough to activate Shea's gag reflex. Instinctively she started to pull back, but Sir Stephen's hand, which had remained on the back of her head, held her in place.

"Work through it, S," he said. "Accept the gift of your Master's cock."

Shea struggled to swallow the saliva that had pooled in her open mouth. Her jaw was tired and her knees ached. She was ready to move on to something else, but apparently that wasn't an option. Trying to harness her submissive grace, Shea inched her head forward to take in more of the huge, hard shaft.

She gagged again, but managed not to rear back, the gentle pressure of Sir Stephen's hand helping her to remain in place. This time, when Master Zach thrust slowly forward, Shea was able to accommodate his girth without gagging. He continued to move forward until the head of his cock pushed past her soft palate and made contact with the back of her throat.

This time she did gag. Sir Stephen held her in place both with his hand on the back of her head, and his words. "Stay with it, S. Try not to resist your Master's will. Focus on acceptance and submission. This is where you belong, naked and on your knees, your Master's cock down your throat."

The truth of Sir Stephen's words resonated in Shea's core, pulling a moan from somewhere deep inside her. She opened her eyes, focusing them for a moment on Sir Stephen, who looked down at her with an intense stare, as if he were willing her with every particle of his being to succeed. She shifted her gaze from Sir Stephen to Master Zach, whose eyes were closed, lips parted, his face a study in raw desire.

Yes, this was where she belonged. This was exactly where she needed to be.

Master Zach reached for Shea's face, cupping her cheekbones with his palms. He began to move, pulling his cock from her throat and then slowly pushing it back again.

Her hands clasped tightly behind her back, Shea struggled to keep her mouth open. Tears were streaming down her cheeks, though she wasn't crying. After a while, she stopped gagging every time he thrust forward. She even managed to lick and suckle at her Master's shaft as it moved back and forth across her tongue.

She forgot the fatigue in her jaw and the ache in her knees. She became aware of the pulse at her clit and the tingle in her throbbing, engorged nipples.

Master Zach groaned softly, his fingers twisting in her hair as he began to thrust, still gently but with more urgency.

"Good," Sir Stephen urged, his hand still a comforting presence on the back of her head. "You can use your hands again. Stroke your Master's balls as you worship his cock."

Shea reached eagerly for Master Zach's balls, which were heavy and warm in her hand. Instinctively, she gripped the base of his shaft in one hand as she gently caressed his heavy, warm balls with her other.

Master Zach moaned again, louder this time, his breath quickening. He stiffened suddenly, his fingers tightening in her hair. Then he gasped, his fingers loosened, his hands falling away.

Suddenly Shea's mouth was flooded with salty, bitter goo. With a startled cry, she dropped her hands and jerked back, sputtering and choking.

Sir Stephen's hand fell away as Master Zach's eyes flew open, his lips parting in surprise. "Sorry about that," he said a little breathlessly, a broad grin moving over his face. "That just sort of snuck up on me."

Confused and dismayed, not sure if she was in trouble or not, Shea glanced from Master Zach to Sir Stephen as she tried to wipe away some of the ejaculate that dribbled down her chin.

Sir Stephen, too, was smiling, though he was also shaking his head. "A properly trained submissive is always ready to receive her Master's offering," he said. "Spitting it out and wiping it off as you have done would be definite grounds for serious punishment."

Shea's heart constricted at his words, her breath catching in her throat.

But, to her relief, he continued, "Obviously, you're not yet properly trained. In fact, you did better than I expected for the first time." He drew his hand suggestively over the substantial bulge in his briefs. "And lucky for you, you've got a second chance. We'll take a little break so you can wash up, and then you will report back here, naked and on your knees, ready to try again, this time with me. Does that suit you, S?"

"Yes, Sir Stephen," she said, surprised to discover she meant it.

"You look absolutely fantastic, Shea. I'm horribly jealous. Clearly, whatever you've been into this past month agrees with you." Katie Anderson, Shea's closest friend and the only one of her vanilla friends who *might* be open-minded enough to accept Shea's new lifestyle without totally freaking out, pulled Shea into a warm embrace.

As they moved toward a booth in their favorite pizza joint, Katie continued, "It's about time we reconnected. I get it that you're totally into this guy, but surely you have to come up for air occasionally. You've missed four happy hours and three movies." She laughed, but then frowned. "If I wasn't so happy for you, I'd be pissed off."

"I know, I know," Shea said ruefully as they sat down opposite one another. "Mea culpa. I've been a horrible friend. It's just been so...so all encompassing, you know?"

Katie nodded, but obviously she didn't know the half of it—she couldn't know. A waitress appeared with two glasses of water and some menus. Once she'd gone, Katie leaned forward conspiratorially. "So tell me everything. Enough with the cryptic texts and the evasions. Is this guy an international spy or something? If you tell me about what he does, you'll have to kill me?"

Shea laughed and then blew out a breath as she tried to think what, and how much, to say. "I know I've been really vague, and I appreciate the space you and the girls have given me. If I tell you what's been going on, I don't want you to tell the others. I just don't think they could really deal with it. I have to warn you. This isn't a typical relationship."

"You're making me nervous, Shea. If I couldn't see that you're obviously happy, I might think this guy was keeping you prisoner in his dungeon or something."

Shea, who had just taken a sip of her water, choked slightly and set the glass down harder than she meant. Did Katie already know? How?

"What?" Katie demanded, lifting her eyebrows. "You looked shocked. I was just kidding, obviously."

"Oh," Shea answered lamely as she tried to gather her thoughts. "It's just, like I said, uh, not typical."

"I *got* that," Katie said, clearly a little exasperated. She put her hands flat on the table and said emphatically, "Now, out with it. The whole story. I promise—no judgments. We're BFFs, remember?"

Shea nodded, smiling to cover her hesitation. She was given a short reprieve by the return of the waitress. They ordered a pizza and mugs of root beer. As soon as the waitress had gone, Katie persisted. "I'm waiting. Tell me everything."

"Okay," Shea said, making a decision. If Katie freaked out, then she freaked out. "First of all, it's not just one guy. It's two."

Katie's eyebrows lifted in surprise. "Two?"

Shea nodded. "I met them at Hardcore, a BDSM club," she said, her heart knocking against her ribs.

Katie's eyebrows disappeared under her bangs, her mouth falling open.

Slowly, hesitantly, Shea began to talk.

It was hard to believe a month had already passed since that fateful night in July when Shea had taken a chance with the two wonderful men who now consumed her world. Though she had yet to stay the night, Shea trained with her Masters at least five times each week. If they were training other subs on the off days or while she was at work, they never mentioned it and she didn't ask, not sure she wanted to know.

While she still had a long way to go, Shea was learning, slowly but surely, how to be a proper submissive. She loved to worship her men's cocks and balls. While she still sometimes worried she might gag or spit, she had learned to open her throat, and usually managed to swallow with reasonable grace, and no longer minded the taste. She thrilled to the ritual and adored the exquisite sense of submissive vulnerability coupled with the empowering feeling of bringing each of her Masters to orgasm.

Her Masters introduced her to levels of erotic pain she would never have believed she could tolerate. She had been welted by the cane, whipped with a single tail, tightly bound in difficult positions for extended periods and paddled until her ass was bruised.

They had worked with her on orgasm responsiveness and denial, bringing her again and again to the edge and then jerking her back with a smack or searing stroke of the whip applied directly to her throbbing clit.

Though it didn't happen every time, if she was lucky, at the end of a training session her Masters would take her up to the second floor. There they would make love to her until she lay nearly unconscious with bliss.

Because they saw her so often, they no longer gave her tasks to perform during the day while away from them, preferring instead to train her directly. Though she was sometimes tempted late at night alone in her bed, she never, ever touched herself, saving her body and her orgasms for the men who owned her.

She had discovered a new ability to concentrate at work, and was more productive than ever. Her efforts didn't go unnoticed, and she had recently been made head of a new research and development team that was working on some very innovative products for a high-end cosmetic company.

An unexpected but welcome byproduct of her newfound happiness was the change in her appetites and cravings. Her work pants had begun to bag, gaping at the waist and sagging at the buttocks. Blouses that used to strain at the buttons now hung loosely on her frame. When she finally found the courage to step on the scale, she had been delighted to see that seventeen pounds had miraculously melted away.

She treated herself to a new wardrobe, adding dresses and tailored skirts to her work ensemble, no longer hiding behind the drab, boxy outfits she used to favor, and buying sexy little sundresses and clingy outfits for her off hours that she never would have dreamed of wearing in her past life.

The guys in the lab, even the dreaded Jeff, began to treat her differently. Aaron and a guy from accounting had even asked her out, though of course she'd said no. People teased her that being in love suited her. They didn't know the half of it.

Whenever she went into the women's bathroom, she couldn't resist lifting her skirt in front of the mirror to admire the bruises and welts that remained from whatever delicious session her Masters and she had engaged in the night before. Aware her vanilla friends and colleagues would be horrified, she felt only pride and a deep sense of satisfaction at her well-earned badges of submissive courage.

Occasionally she sensed a little friction between the guys, which she was pretty sure revolved around her, but they were careful never to make her feel uncomfortable or conflicted. Sometimes she wondered where things were going, and how long they could sustain the dynamic that existed between them. No one ever threw around words like love, for which she was grateful. She had all she could handle at this point.

The pizza arrived, but neither of them touched it as Shea related her story and Katie listened, open-mouthed. Shea gave her an edited, much-diluted version that was heavy on the romantic side and rather vague in terms of specifics, especially regarding the BDSM training, but still it was more than enough to shock her friend into stunned silence.

Shea gave a self-conscious laugh and nodded toward the pie. "Aren't you hungry?" She took a slice and placed it on her plate, though she herself had no appetite, her stomach clenched with nervous anticipation of Katie's reaction.

Katie, too, took a slice, lifting it to her mouth for a bite.

"So?" Shea said anxiously, "You're totally freaked out, right?"

Katie nodded, and Shea's heart sank. She wiped her lips with her napkin. "Yeah. I guess I am. Definitely not my flavor." But then she added with an impish grin, "But I also think it's one of the sexiest, most exciting things I've ever heard. Holy shit, it's like that book, you know that *Fifty Shades* whatever thing, except this is even better, because you have *two* guys!" She shook her head in wonder. "Shea Anne O'Connor, you are *amazing*. I am in awe."

Shea laughed with relief. "Seriously? You're okay with it?"

"Sure. Like I said—not my thing, but so what? You're happy, right?"

"More than happy."

"Then that's all that matters."

Chapter 9

Shea came over to see the guys early on a Saturday morning in late August, armed with a box of fruit pastries and blueberry muffins. The three of them were enjoying a casual breakfast out on the porch when Steve's cell chirped in his pocket.

He reached for it and glanced at the screen. "Oh, cool," he said to Zach. "Tag is hosting a bonfire tonight at his place. He's going to debut those LED whips we've been working on."

Turning to Shea, Steve added, "They're like fire whips, but we use LED technology instead of fuel and flame. The whips are made from hollow plastic tubes with LED circuitry fitted inside."

"Except it's not just a conventional LED string," Zach said enthusiastically. "Steve's modest about it, but he's really good with electricity, and he figured out how to design circuitry that offers more strength and flexibility."

"We had a breakthrough this week," Steve said, looking pleased. "It gets kind of complicated, but in simple terms, we fill the tubes with liquid to protect the circuitry. Tag was taking it to an electrician friend of his for some tweaking. He must have given the thumbs up."

"That sounds really interesting," Shea said, her scientific interest piqued. "How does that—"

Steve's phone chirped again, and he glanced down, cutting her off. "Ah, even better. He says it's not just any bonfire. It's a BDSM bonfire. In addition to the demo, they'll have a casual play party for a few close friends. He wants us to come, and says to bring whomever we like. Of course we'd want to bring you, Shea. It's more than high time you met our friends and took your rightful place as our sub girl."

"Oh," Shea said softly. *Our sub girl.* She quite liked the sound of that.

"The play at these events is usually pretty intense, but we'd be with you every step of the way. Would you be up for that?" Zach asked.

"Am I ready?" Shea asked, suddenly apprehensive at the thought of other people in the scene witnessing her submission. The cloak of her recently acquired submissive serenity slipped a bit. What if she got nervous and made a fool of herself?

"If we didn't think you were up to it, we wouldn't have suggested it," Steve said gently, fixing her with that intense gaze that always made her tumble headlong into his dark blue eyes.

Of course, he was right. She would trust her Masters. If they thought she was ready, then she was.

"Thank you, Sir Stephen. Thank you, Master Zach. Your sub girl would love to go."

After leaving the guys that morning, Shea drove straight to the Clara's Naughty Toys BDSM boutique, which was located in the same block as the club. Along with Taggart Fitzgerald's invitation to the party that night, he had requested that the guys come in for an extra shift that afternoon, as he was up against a deadline for a big order.

Not for the first time, Shea wondered what it might be like to live full-time with her Masters. The thought was at once intriguing and frightening. Though she already spent most of her free time with them, the knowledge that she still had her own place to return to was comforting. Or was it a way to maintain her distance; to stop herself from getting too close?

Whatever the case, today she had things to do—her most important task of which was to get something sexy to wear for that evening's festivities.

Shea had been inside the boutique before, but only to stare at the myriad erotic torture implements, sex toys and clothing offered for sale. A woman on a mission, she now went directly to the clothing racks. She flicked her way through the items until she found the perfect black corset. She selected several sizes and took them into the dressing room, a single large space lined with mirrors.

There were two other people already in there, one of them a woman in her thirties trying on a long black, satin gown with slits high up on the thighs, the other woman naked save for a pair of thong panties. She was maybe fifty but very fit, and she was holding up several different tiny camisoles in front of the mirror. Shea resisted the impulse to tell her they would never fit over her surgically augmented breasts.

She went to an unoccupied corner of the room and, turning her back on the other two women, quickly shucked her clothing, including her bra. She started to reach for the largest of the three sizes, but instead selected the smallest.

It had three vertical rows of hook-and-eye closures. Shea sucked in her stomach as she hooked the dozen tiny closures into place and then adjusted herself into the built-in, very low cut bra. The corset cinched her tightly around the waist, lifting her breasts high and cradling them together to form a deep cleavage. She stared at herself in the mirror, transfixed by the hourglass figure the outfit had created. The fit was extremely snug, but she quite liked the feeling. It was akin to bondage, reminding her of the ropes her Masters used to bind her. She loved the way it held her tight, making her feel instantly sexy and submissive.

"Whoa," the younger of the two women said from behind her. She saw in the mirror that both of the women were staring at her, approving looks on their faces.

"Honey, that thing was made for you," the other woman said. "You look super hot."

Shea turned to smile at the women. "Thanks," she said, feeling a little shy, but very pleased. "I'm wearing it to a party tonight."

She wanted to wear it out of the store, but figured she had better buy it first. She was taken aback by the hefty price tag, but decided she deserved it. It was a gift to herself, and to her Masters.

Once back at her apartment building, Shea stopped at the communal mailboxes and pulled out the usual assortment of junk mail and bills from her box, which she stuffed into her purse.

She passed the afternoon by writing up a few lab reports on some recent experiments her team had been conducting on non-greasy emollients, and emptying out her closet and bureau, piling up for donation old clothing she would never wear again.

She grilled a piece of salmon and made a small salad for dinner, and then brushed her teeth and took another shower, carefully grooming herself in preparation for the evening. She even painted her fingernails and toenails, something she hadn't done in years.

Finally, she put on the sexy corset and added a long, flowing wrap-around black skirt. She chose a pretty cream-colored lace shawl for cover, and in case it got chilly at the bonfire. She tried on the sexy four-inch heels she'd worn for her debut at Hardcore, but figured she'd be safer in kitten heels, since the event was being held outside. She wasn't sure what to expect, but whatever it was, she was determined to make Sir Stephen and Master Zach proud.

Shea sat on the blanket between her Masters at the bonfire, her fingers wrapped around a mug of hot apple cider spiced with cinnamon and cloves. On their right were Matt and Bonnie Wilson, on their left Liam and Allie Byrne.

The two couples had already been out back getting the fire going when Steve, Zach and she had arrived at Taggart Fitzgerald's house. Taggart made a very imposing figure, as tall and broad as Zach, with deep-set, brooding eyes and rugged, craggy features, his skin the tan of someone who had spent much of his life outdoors.

Rylee Miller, Taggart's live-in lover, full-time submissive and business partner, had been extremely welcoming, putting Shea instantly at ease. A few years younger than Shea, she was a beautiful woman, with eyes an unusual shade of blue that exactly matched the soft leather sub collar she wore at her throat.

If Shea had been shy about wearing her revealing corset to the party, Rylee's outfit had made her look positively overdressed. Rylee, like Shea, had large breasts, but the rest of her body was that of an athlete—her shoulders broad, her hips narrow, her ass small and muscular, her legs long and lean. She looked like a Greek goddess in the white, diaphanous gown she wore, which clung to her curves, widening into a skirt that swirled loosely around her ankles, her feet clad in thin-strapped white sandals. The back of the gown was cut so low that her entire back was bare, and it was evident that, beneath the sheer, nearly translucent fabric of her dress, Rylee was naked.

Though Shea had been initially shy, Taggart and Rylee had both been so welcoming that she had felt instantly at ease. When they all went out back to meet the others, they, too, were friendly and warm, no one batting an eye when Sir Stephen and Master Zach presented Shea as their shared submissive.

All eyes now turned to Taggart, who stood several yards away in a clearing. He held a lit wooden match to the end of a long, white, braided whip. As the fuel-soaked cotton and Kevlar whip ignited, a line of fire whooshed up its length, drawing a collective gasp of appreciation from all seated around the bonfire.

He began to wave the fiery whip in graceful spirals all around his body and over his head. Shea stared, mesmerized by the breathtaking dance of the undulating, coiling snake of fire. The core of the flame was a bright white-yellow, but as it twisted and arced through the air, reds, oranges, golds and even deep blues and greens flashed and sparkled in the dark—a mini Aurora Borealis beneath the dark Oregon sky.

Shea was disappointed when, after a few minutes, the fiery whip died into the darkness. After a moment of silence, everyone began to talk at once, amidst a scatter of appreciative applause.

Taggart moved back near the bonfire and made a little bow. Straightening, he said, "Now I have something really exciting to show you all. Zach, Steve and I have been working on this prototype for a couple of months now, and I think we finally have something we can offer for sale in our catalog."

He turned to Rylee, who rose and moved toward a large bag set some distance from the bonfire. Returning to Taggart, she handed him what looked like a single tail whip and a flogger, except instead of leather, they appeared to be made of flexible, clear plastic.

Taggart held up the two impact toys and said, "These are light whips. Unlike fire whips, they actually do more than entertain. And here's the fun part." He flicked both his wrists and the toys suddenly lit up, like those light bracelets you got at amusement parks.

The effect was beautiful, if less flashy than actual fire. As he cracked the glowing whip and waved the lighted flogger, it looked in the dark as if he were flicking a comet's tail in one hand, a handle sprouting glow-in-the-dark, undulating sea grass in the other.

"They're beautiful," Allie breathed.

"I want one of each," Matt and Bonnie said at exactly the same time, causing everyone, including them, to laugh.

Taggart announced, "I'm going to demonstrate the beauty of this single tail on my lovely sub girl, Rylee. I need volunteers for the flogger." As he said this, Taggart looked pointedly at Sir Stephen, who gave a brisk nod.

A jolt of terrified delight hurtled its way through Shea's gut. She sent a silent plea to the BDSM gods to lend her submissive courage and grace, since at that precise moment, she had neither.

Sir Stephen rose to his feet and extended his hand, the invitation clear. He hadn't asked her, but then, he didn't need to. Shea belonged to Sir Stephen and to Master Zach. That, the gods whispered in reminder, was all she needed to hang on to.

Master Zach's deep, comforting voice sounded in her ear. "You can do this, S. You are our brave, beautiful girl. Make us proud tonight."

His words melted the lump of anxiety that had risen in her throat. Leaving her shawl with Master Zach, Shea took Sir Stephen's hand and allowed him to pull her upright.

Sir Stephen and Taggart led Rylee and Shea several feet away from the bonfire, though not as far away as Taggart had stood for his fire whip display. Shea was glad for the partial cover of the darkness.

As she turned to Rylee, the other woman plucked at the thin straps that held up her gown and slid them down her arms. She let the dress puddle in a pool at her feet so she was standing naked, save for small gold hoops that glittered at her nipples.

Naked!

Shea glanced toward Sir Stephen, but he was conferring with Taggart, their heads bent close and turned away from Shea. She looked to Master Zach for direction and support. He smiled at her and lifted one thumb in encouragement.

Aware all eyes were on her, Shea girded her courage as she reached for the sash that held her skirt in place. As Rylee had done, she let the skirt fall away. She glanced anxiously toward Sir Stephen, hoping he would somehow indicate she had done enough.

No such luck.

He whirled his index finger in a circle at her, the gesture indicating she was to continue.

Shea began to unhook her corset with trembling fingers. When she got to the bottom hook, the corset sprang open and fell away from her body, her large, heavy breasts tumbling out for everyone to see. Her heart was beating so loudly she was sure everyone could hear it as she slipped her fingers beneath the elastic straps that held her panties in place, and pushed them down her legs.

Resisting the impulse to cover her body with her arms, Shea glanced once more at Rylee, who was standing with her shoulders back, her expression serene. Shea, who had unconsciously hunched forward, tried to copy both her posture and her demeanor, though she couldn't stop the scorching heat that moved over her cheeks.

Taggart and Sir Stephen approached the two naked women, each moving to stand beside his girl. "You're beautiful," Sir Stephen whispered in Shea's ear. Though she remained nervous, his words warmed her and brought a smile to her lips.

"For this demonstration," Taggart said, addressing Rylee and Shea, "We want you to face each other so you're in profile to the bonfire. Stand about three feet apart and take each other's hands."

Rylee and Shea turned to each other as instructed. Rylee held out her hands for Shea to take. As she looked up into the face of the taller girl, she was surprised to see Rylee's cheeks were as pink as hers felt, her smile shy. For the first time, it occurred to Shea that this might be hard for Rylee too, however gracefully she presented herself. The thought gave her courage, and she gave Rylee's hands a friendly squeeze. Rylee's smile broadened, and she squeezed back.

Sir Stephen moved behind Shea as Taggart took his place behind Rylee. Sir Stephen leaned in close from behind, his mouth near Shea's ear. "I want you to exult in your erotic suffering tonight, S. Offer it as your gift to our friends." As he spoke, he lifted her hair and gently pushed it over her shoulders, baring her back for the flogger.

Though she remained nervous, his touch and his words had the effect of a soothing balm, and the worst of her jitteriness eased away. "Yes, Sir Stephen. Thank you, Sir."

"We begin," Taggart said in his gruff, gravelly voice. He snapped his wrist and the single tail in his hand once again lit up like something out of a Star Wars movie. Though Shea couldn't see, she assumed Sir Stephen had also activated the flogger.

Without preamble, Taggart flicked the tip of the single tail behind Rylee, the punctuation of its lighted tip against flesh unmistakable. Rylee barely registered the impact, save for the slight press of her lips.

At the same time, the flogger brushed against her back. It wasn't the soft, suede caress she was used to, but more of a stingy slap.

Holding hands with Rylee as they faced each other, Shea felt the kinship, as if she and Rylee were sister subs. The idea appealed to her. Here was a potential new girlfriend, a kindred soul who not only understood and accepted her deep-seated submissive longings but embraced them as her own.

Sir Stephen's stroke was light against her shoulders and back, a pleasant stinging sensation that warmed her skin. Taggart expertly flicked his whip in a flowing arc behind Rylee, the light moving in graceful curves, the tip snapping upon impact with Rylee's flesh.

Rylee's lips had compressed into a thin line. She blinked rapidly in an effort to maintain her composure, holding tightly to Shea's hands. Shea squeezed back in sympathy, aware Rylee was taking a much more intense whipping than she was.

The first hard stroke came against Shea's ass, landing with a resounding crash against both ass cheeks like a dozen hard palms. Shea, who had been focused on Rylee, gave a startled cry of pain and surprise. Sir Stephen began to flog her in earnest, the hard plastic tresses smashing relentlessly against her ass, the tips sometimes curling painfully around her hips like strokes of pure fire.

Shea bit down hard on her lower lip and squeezed Rylee's hands in her effort to maintain her grace and silence. It took every ounce of her will not to twist away from the relentless onslaught. Not for the first time, Shea wondered why she had such a need for the erotic pain her Masters gave her. Why did she crave this suffering? What was it about it that ultimately filled the emptiness she had always felt deep in her soul?

While Sir Stephen was hitting her just as hard as a moment before, she found she was able to tolerate it better. Somehow, she had harnessed the fear and the pain. She could handle whatever he meted out. More than that, she wanted it.

She focused again on Rylee, who was trembling, her grip tight on Shea's fingers as her Master's lighted whip crisscrossed her back and thighs. She had risen on her toes and she was trembling, beads of perspiration visible on her upper lip.

Then, the most amazing thing began to happen. All at once, Rylee's bone-crushing grip eased. Her shoulders, which had risen in her effort to handle the pain, relaxed, her feet settling flat against the ground. Her eyes closed, and her head fell slowly back, her chin lifting so she was facing the star-studded sky.

"Yes," Taggart breathed from behind her. "Yes."

Shea watched with awe, more than just a witness to Rylee's

submissive journey, but a part of it.

Gradually she became aware that the flogging behind her had slowed, the intensity decreased as the crashing plastic eased into a swish against her stinging skin.

Taggart, too, was easing his stroke. Rylee remained still as a statue, her face lifted to the sky, her lips parted as if in silent prayer. When Shea let go of Rylee's hands, Rylee's arms fell limply to her sides.

Sir Stephen's arms encircled Shea from behind, his strong body pressed against her back as he held her. She leaned into him, though she was unable to tear her eyes away from the scene. She understood Rylee was flying, a term she'd come across in her research but hadn't really comprehended, until now.

Finally Taggart lowered his whip and set it, still glowing, on the ground. Bending his tall frame slightly, he placed one hand behind Rylee's back, the other behind her knees, and lifted the naked girl into his arms.

Rylee startled, as if awakening from an enchanted sleep, and then smiled dreamily up at her master. He lowered his head to kiss her and everyone around the campfire broke into spontaneous, joyous laughter and applause.

Master Zach appeared beside Shea, and Sir Stephen stepped back to allow him to wrap a shawl around Shea's shoulder. Together, they led Shea back to the bonfire.

As she settled between them on the blanket, Bonnie leaned over to her with a warm smile. "You were fantastic, Shea. I was so jealous watching you. I'm so glad Sir Stephen and Master Zach have found such a wonderful woman."

Warmth suffused Shea at Bonnie's kind words. She smiled shyly, an enormous happiness filling her with such lightness she might have floated away, save for the anchoring touch of the men on either side of her.

Her eyes fell on Taggart and Rylee, who now sat on the other side of the fire, Rylee still cradled in Taggart's lap, her face still suffused with a kind of inner light.

"That was amazing, watching her transform like that," Shea said.

"It's called flying," Sir Stephen said, affirming what Shea had surmised. "It's a kind of altered state of being it's possible to achieve through intense erotic pain."

"Bonnie calls it Nirvana," Matt, who had obviously overhead, said.

"That's right," Bonnie agreed. "A state characterized by freedom from or oblivion to pain, worry, and the external world."

"Can anyone fly?" Shea asked, deeply intrigued. "Even me?"

Master Zach's arm came around Shea's shoulder. "Absolutely you," he said. "That's a promise."

~*~

It was well after midnight when Steve pulled the Audi into their driveway alongside Shea's car. Zach and Shea, who had fallen asleep in the backseat with their heads touching, both opened their eyes as he turned off the engine.

As they climbed out of the car, Zach said, "One of us should follow you home to make sure you get there safely."

"No, that's okay," Shea replied with a shake of her head. "I'm fine, really. I can text you when I get there. I'm a big girl." She flashed a smile.

"You sure?" Zach said. "It's no trouble."

"Absolutely certain," she assured him.

"Okay, you text us the second you pull into the parking lot," Zach said.

"And again once you're safely in your apartment," Steve added.

"I will, I will," Shea promised with a laugh.

Zach took her into his arms, wrapping her in a big bear hug. When he let her go, Steve hugged her, suddenly aware he had yet to kiss this girl on the lips. Had she been any other trainee, that wouldn't have been remarkable at all. Both Zach and he were careful about keeping anything that smacked of romance out of their relationships with their trainees, but Shea wasn't any other trainee—not by a long shot.

Especially after tonight, Steve could no longer pretend to himself that he wasn't falling hard for this girl. Instead of freaking out over it, he had to admit he was happy. Since the debacle with Sandra, he'd been holding himself back, keeping his heart firmly under wraps. Yet, somehow, Shea had slipped in when he wasn't looking, and there was no denying it.

As he let Shea go, he glanced at Zach, wondering if he, too, were falling for Shea. And if he was, would he admit it? It was interesting that both Shea and Zach claimed to share the same horror of the *drama* that relationships entailed, and yet both of them continued to move forward in this triad of exploration with as much eagerness as he.

Shea stepped back and pulled her purse from her shoulder. Reaching in, she took out her keys. As she opened her car door and slipped into the driver's seat, she looked up at them with a radiant smile. "Tonight was one of the most amazing nights of my life," she said with sweet sincerity. "Thank you for introducing me to your friends."

"You were wonderful," Zach said as Steve nodded his agreement.

"Don't forget to text," Steve reminded her.

"Yes, Sir, I promise I won't forget," Shea replied, still smiling. She left the car door ajar as she turned the key in the ignition.

Nothing happened.

She knitted her brows and turned the key again.

Still nothing.

"Shit," she swore softly.

Steve placed his hand on the door and leaned down. "What is it?"

"My stupid car won't start." She blew out a breath and then closed her eyes, her lips moving as if she were saying a prayer. She turned the key again, to no avail.

"It's late," Zach said, stepping forward. "One of us can give you a ride home. I'll have a look at the car in the morning. Hopefully it's something simple like the battery."

"That's crazy," Steve interjected. "Why don't you just stay here tonight? We have an extra bedroom. Or even better," he added before he could stop himself, "we could all three sleep in my bed."

Zach shot him a look, and Steve offered an answering shrug, aware he was pushing forward his new internal agenda of bringing their as yet unacknowledged relationship more into the open. The words had sprung from his lips before he could stop himself, but really, it only made sense. It wasn't like the three of them hadn't spent plenty of hours in his bedroom already.

"Oh, I couldn't," Shea began.

Steve was ready to assure her that she could, but to his pleased surprise, Zach got there first. "Sure you could. That's a great idea. We'll all pile into Steve's bed. It's not like we haven't been there before."

Shea looked from Steve to Zach and then back to Steve. "Well, if you're sure..."

Steve reached for Shea's hand and helped her out of her car. "We're sure."

They went directly upstairs to get ready for bed, Zach stopping at his room while Steve and Shea headed down the hall to the master bedroom. Steve found a spare toothbrush for Shea to use, and he stole sidelong glances at her as they washed up side-by-side at the double sinks in his bathroom.

Both naked, Shea and he climbed into bed. Steve sensed Shea's nervousness, her movements a little stiff, uncertainty in her face. To calm her, he pulled her into his arms and kissed the top of her head as they settled beneath the covers. Despite his fatigue, his cock hardened at the presence of the naked girl beside him.

The rest of him, however, began to sink at once into the mattress, as if leaden weights had been attached to his limbs. It was a struggle just to keep his eyes open.

Zach appeared in the doorway, still in his boxer shorts. "Mind if I join you?" Without waiting for a reply, he stripped off his boxers and quickly slipped beneath the sheets.

He scooted toward them, spooning Shea from the back, his arm flung loosely over her body.

Steve, lying on his back with Shea snuggled against him, reached with his free hand for the bedside lamp and clicked off the light.

~*~

Zach opened his eyes, uncertain for a moment where he was. He was on his back, his left arm pinned beneath something. Turning his head, he saw the bright red tumble of Shea's hair and smelled the lingering, warm vanilla scent of her perfume. He extricated his arm carefully from beneath her body and lifted himself on one elbow.

Steve was on his side, his back to them, snoring softly. Shea lay on her back, her face turned away. The sheet had slipped down and covered only her lower half, leaving her large, lovely breasts bare.

Zach waited for the sensation of being trapped that always clanged down over him like the bars of a cage whenever he broke his own rules and woke up in someone else's bed, but it didn't come. Oddly, despite his longstanding promise to himself to always wake up alone, lying here beside his two best friends felt like the most natural thing in the world.

When had that happened? When had Shea moved from trainee to their personal submissive to a true friend? However it had happened, instead of freaking him out, the realization made Zach happy. Smiling, he reached over and drew a circle around Shea's nipple, which instantly stiffened to his touch.

Shea turned her head, her eyes opening sleepily and then widening as if in shock. A hand came to her mouth, and then understanding seem to dawn as she, too, recalled where she was.

She smiled at Zach and held out her arms.

The gesture was so simple and so compelling that Zach moved at once to take her into his embrace. His morning erection was like an iron bar between them as he lifted himself over her. It occurred to him he could fuck her then and there. Steve slept like the dead, and anyway, the memory foam mattress transferred almost no motion. You could jump up and down on one side of the darn thing and not even feel it on the other. Better yet, they no longer had to use condoms, since Shea had informed them a few weeks back, blushing adorably as she did so, that she'd gone on birth control pills and was now protected.

Shea's breasts were soft and yielding against his chest. He reached between her legs, his fingers seeking her soft, wet heat. To his surprise, she slid from beneath him. "Please let me serve you, Master Zach," she whispered.

Without waiting for his reply, she slipped from beneath him and pushed at his shoulder, indicating he should lie on his back. While one could argue that her behavior was decidedly un-submissive, it wasn't as if they were in a training session, despite her use of his title. And anyway, he was curious what she had in mind and so allowed her to push him onto his back.

She flashed him a smile that was at once shy and knowing as she crouched beside him and took his shaft into her right hand. Zach glanced toward Steve, who hadn't moved and still continued to snore softly beside them.

Shea opened her pretty lips, her mouth hovering just above Zack's shaft. "Please, Sir, may I worship your cock?"

"Shit, yeah," Zach replied with a grin.

Shea closed her lips over his cock and went eagerly to work. Gone was the tentative, uncertain girl they had met at Hardcore. She was both skilled and enthusiastic as she stroked, licked, sucked and massaged his cock and balls.

It wasn't long before an orgasm gathered itself inside him. He lightly touched the top of her head, an unspoken signal between them that he was about to come. She didn't miss a beat as he spurted in several spasms of pure pleasure into her willing mouth.

The sound of Steve's voice startled him. They both looked over to see Steve, who had eyes only for Shea. "Hey there, slave girl," he said, his eyes glinting with lust. "My turn."

After they had finished breakfast down in the kitchen, Zach turned to Shea. "I'll check out your car now. Hopefully it just needs a jump." He looked to Steve. "Want to give me a hand?"

Steve pushed back from the table and stood. "Sure." He glanced at Shea. "Where're the keys?"

"I'll get them." Shea stood and moved toward the hook by the back door where she had hung her purse the night before. Bringing the bag to the table, she opened it and reached inside. "Oh, I forgot all about my mail," she said, taking out several envelopes. "I was so busy yesterday I forgot I even had it in my purse." She set the envelopes on the table and then resumed rummaging for her key. Finding it, she handed it to Zach.

Shea remained in the kitchen to clean up while Zach and Steve went out to see about the car. Zach had Steve sit in the driver seat to pop the hood. "Go ahead and see if it'll start this morning," he said as he locked the hood into an open position.

Steve turned the key. The engine made a loud clunking noise and then went silent. "I don't think it's the battery," Steve called from the car. "The electronics and lights are working inside the car. "

Zach scowled as he pulled the dipstick from the oil tank. "Shit. There's no oil in this thing! I don't know how she's been driving this car at all. It's my educated guess that the engine has seized. She's going to need a new engine, which would cost more than this old junk heap is worth."

They went back inside to tell Shea the bad news, but stopped short when they looked at her face. She was holding a piece of paper in her hands, which were shaking as she stared down at it with wide, disbelieving eyes.

Zach was instantly at her side. "Shea, what is it? What's happened?"

Shea held up the piece of paper. "Thirty days," she said. "It says I have thirty days to vacate. The complex is being turned into condos."

Zach took the paper and scanned it, and then handed it off to Steve. Sitting down next to Shea, he put his arm around her shoulders and pulled her close. "Man, that really stinks, Shea. I know exactly how you're feeling, too, because the same thing happened to me. Don't worry, sweetheart. We're here for you."

Shea managed a wan smile. "Thanks," she said, and then, "What about my car? Were you able to get it started?"

Zach glanced at Steve, who looked up from the letter and shook his head. "Zach says the engine has seized. Apparently you were driving the thing without any oil in it. He doesn't think it's worth fixing."

"I knew about the oil leak," she said in a small, miserable voice. "I've been adding oil every week but…" Her mouth worked as if she was going to say something more, but instead she burst into tears and then hid her face in her hands.

Zach pulled her closer, undone by her tears. "Shh, don't cry, baby. We'll figure this out together."

Steve came to sit on her other side, his face a mask of concern. "The answer's pretty obvious, isn't it, Zach?" he said quietly over the weeping girl's head. "We've been heading this way a while now. This just makes it that much simpler."

All at once, Zach knew he was right. The old tape tried to start up in his head, warning him about the dangers of getting too entangled in the emotional mess relationships always entailed, but he silenced the running loop and nodded his agreement. "I barely use my car. And we have an extra bedroom. She's here all the time anyway."

Steve lifted his eyebrows, as if surprised at Zach's easy agreement, but then nodded vigorously. "The solution's staring us in the face."

Steve reached out to touch Shea's shoulder, and Zach let his arms fall away from her. "Shea, listen to me," Steve said.

Shea lifted her tear-streaked face. "I'm sorry," she said, sniffing. "This is so stupid. I didn't mean to cry."

"It's okay. But you don't need to worry anymore. Zach and I have an idea that will solve your problems. It makes total sense, given that you're always here anyway. This is just the natural next step."

Zach jumped up and grabbed the box of tissues from the counter. Returning to the table, he handed Shea a tissue and slid back into his seat. "Steve and I work and play in the same places. My car mostly sits unused in the garage. There's no reason you couldn't use it to get to work."

"Yeah," Steve said eagerly. "We have a spare bedroom, and I own this place free and clear, so rent isn't an issue."

Shea looked from Steve to Zach and then back to Steve, her brows knitting with apparent confusion, and then her expression changed suddenly, hope lighting her face like a burst of sunlight. "Wait a minute. Are you asking me to move in with you?"

"Why, yes," Steve said with a laugh. "That's exactly what we're doing."

Zach was suddenly unable to speak, the realization of what they'd just set in motion smacking him like a sucker punch to the gut. What had he just agreed to?

CHAPTER 10

Steve had been uncertain how things might shake out between the three of them once Shea moved in, given both Zach's and Shea's lack of experience with live-in lovers. Zach had seemed a little dazed at first, but when Steve had tried to feel him out on the subject, he'd been evasive, assuring Steve everything was fine and dandy. Overall, things seemed to be going pretty smoothly.

In the two weeks since she'd been fully ensconced with them, they continued to train in the dungeon as they had been, and to take her upstairs afterward for lovemaking.

Shea mostly slept in her own bedroom, but occasionally she crawled into either Zach's or Steve's bed at night, usually just to snuggle. While Steve was developing rather strong feelings for Shea, he was surprised at his own complete lack of jealousy when it came to the relationship between Zach and Shea. Maybe it was because he felt so close to Zach already, given their unique training relationship, and the fact they'd shared Shea in every respect up to this point.

Of the three of them, Zach seemed to have the most difficulty adjusting. Training sessions continued to go fabulously well, but the intimacy aspects of the relationship were still scary for his friend. When Steve tried to broach the topic, Zach continued to insist the triad was a Master/sub/Master connection, rather than two guys falling in love with the same girl.

"I don't do love," Zach had announced at one point during the first week as they were driving home from work.

"What does that even mean, Zach?" Steve had countered. "It's not something you *do*. It's something that happens between people with a particularly intense connection like the three of us share." More gently, he'd added, "Look, I know this relationship stuff is scary for you and Shea, but you're both doing really well with it. It's happening naturally. The only thing you have to do is stop fighting it. Accept that we three have something special—something amazing—and stop trying to pigeonhole it into some relationship thing."

"You're right, Steve," Zach had admitted in a moment of candor. "I don't want to fuck this up. I just get scared sometimes, you know? I'm not used to this stuff. I'm still feeling my way, I guess."

"We all are," Steve had agreed. "As long as we keep doing it together, we'll be okay. I promise."

Shea had fit in well with their friends, none of whom had batted an eye at the concept of the two of them sharing a sub. A week after the bonfire, they had gone with Tag and Rylee to dinner and then to Hardcore. Matt Wilson had invited them to his private club, Paradise Found, of which Liam and Allie Byrne were also members, giving Shea a chance to get to know their friends better, as well as get more comfortable with group scenes.

The dinner out with Shea's friend, Katie, and her boyfriend, a likable but rather dull guy named Stan, had been a little strange, as the vanilla couple clearly tried to pretend they were totally fine with what Stan kept calling "your wild and crazy threesome." The get-together had been Shea's idea, however, and Steve and Zach had both agreed they didn't want to cut her off from her previous life, if she wanted to remain connected.

Shea had warned them in advance that, while Katie knew they were a triad, and was vaguely aware of their BDSM involvement, she and Stan were fairly conservative. Zach and he had been on their best behavior, despite joking with Shea in advance that they might require her to suck their cocks under the table and to address them as Master and Sir in her vanilla friends' presence.

Shea's birthday was coming up, and Zach and he had begun discussing how they might celebrate. They'd come up with an idea they ran by Shea that evening after work.

"We're going to have a small birthday celebration, a dinner party," Zach said, introducing the topic.

Shea immediately shook her head, as Steve had thought she might. "I don't really like birthday parties," she said. "At least not where I'm the center of attention."

"It's not about what you like, S," Steve said, slipping easily into his dominant persona. "It's about what pleases your Masters. You belong to us and it pleases us to honor you in this way. If it's uncomfortable for you to be the center of attention, then that's precisely where our focus should be. You'll learn to harness your discomfort and your fear, the same way you did with the cane."

Steve's cock hardened at the memory of Shea's initial cane training. Though she could now handle a pretty intense caning, that first time had been a struggle. She had resisted out of fear—she had seen videos online, she told them, of women brutally marked with vicious, bloody welts.

Zach, in that soothing way he had, had reminded her she was safe in their experienced hands. Though she'd remained afraid, she'd agreed to submit without further protest.

They'd had her stand upright for her first caning, since bending over tightened the muscles, making the experience more painful. To keep her centered and in position, they'd suspended her wrists from the ceiling chains. Zach had stood in front of her, stroking her breasts, tweaking her nipples and rubbing her cunt to keep her relaxed. Steve had started slowly, warming her skin with a steady, light tap to get her used to the feel and sound of the cane.

How he loved the power rush evoked by that first whimper of pain, the startled yelps of fear that segued into moans of raw lust. He craved the control aspect of BDSM, exulting in his ability as a Dom to reduce an independent, strong woman to a quivering, gasping sub girl who begged him for more. It fed his soul to guide her to that sacred, mysterious place where pleasure and pain melded together into something so much more powerful. Knowing that he was able to give her that, to give her something she could not give herself, satisfied something deep in his dominant core.

By the end of the session, Shea had taken a serious caning, her ass and the backs of her thighs beautifully welted. Zach had been masterful in keeping her centered and reasonably calm as the caning had intensified. As soon as they released her wrists, the girl fell spontaneously to her knees and begged them to allow her to worship their cocks in thanks.

Talk about a win-win situation, Steve now mused with a smile.

"Remember that video you made for us when we first met you?" Zach said. "Remember how in your fantasy you were passed from man to man, forced to take whatever they gave you?"

Color had seeped into Shea's cheeks, but at the same time her eyes softened, her features relaxing with what Steve thought of as submissive serenity. "Yes, Master Zach. I remember," she breathed.

"We plan to make your fantasies come true as our birthday gift to you," Sir Stephen said. "Does that suit you, S?"

Shea's color remained high, but her eyes were shining, her lips softly parted. "Yes, Sir. It suits me to a T."

~*~

Shea slipped the short gown over her head, careful not to mess up her hair or makeup. She was both nervous and excited as she dressed for that night's party. While she was thrilled at the thought of having one of her darkest, sexiest fantasies brought to life, she was reminded of the old maxim about being careful what you wished for.

She was glad her new girlfriends would be there with her. While she hadn't consciously separated herself from her old friends, they had naturally drifted apart. Going out to movies and happy hours and giggling over potential mates, movie stars and the latest office gossip no longer held much appeal.

She'd experienced an immediate connection with Rylee, Bonnie and Allie. It had been a kind of homecoming to a place she'd never been but had always missed. She felt like Ayla in that book *The Clan of the Cave Bear*, having spent her entire life with the wrong species. Now, welcomed with open arms by not only Steve and Zach, but by all their friends in the scene, it was as if she had finally found her own people.

She was especially close with Rylee, who, they had discovered in their conversations, had shared a similar out-of-place feeling in the world for much of her life. Rylee shared Shea's early love of *Story of O*, and Shea had been thrilled to discover that the Leather Master, as Taggart was sometimes called, used Rylee's first initial, too, when they were in a scene.

When Shea had confided her anxiety about the upcoming party, Rylee had shared in delicious detail the amazing scene that had taken place at her first birthday with Taggart and his friends the year before. "Trust me," Rylee had assured her. "These guys of ours are the best Doms in the scene, not just in Portland, but anywhere on the planet. Whatever they have planned for you, it'll be amazing."

Calmed by the memory of their conversation, Shea opened her eyes and regarded herself in the bathroom mirror. The guys had presented her with a beautiful white sleeveless gown, the shoulder straps held closed by gold clips. It draped prettily over her breasts like a Greek toga and was gathered at the waist with a gold sash, the skirt falling to just above her knees.

On her feet were flat, gold leather sandals, and in her hair, which she had swept up in a chignon for the occasion, she wore the beautiful gold barrette Allie had given her as an early birthday present. Allie, a jewelry designer by profession, had fashioned what, at first glance, appeared to be an abstract circular design, but on closer inspection was actually a single tail whip coiled in on itself.

A few tendrils of Shea's unruly, red hair had escaped from the barrette, but she didn't bother with them, aware they would only spring free again. She had put on more makeup than usual in honor of the party—red lipstick, gold sparkly eye shadow, mascara and even eyeliner.

As directed by her Masters, she wore nothing beneath her gown, and her nipples were clearly visible. She was no longer self-conscious about her body, and not just because, for the first time in her life, she was at her desired weight. It was more that she had truly surrendered her modesty to her Masters. It pleased them to see her naked and, by extension, this pleased her.

The doorbell rang. Shea rushed from the bathroom and hurried down the stairs to get the door. The guys had warned her to keep out of the kitchen and dining room, instead directing her to greet the guests as they arrived.

Allie and Liam Byrne were at the door. With dark hair and green eyes, Liam, or Sir Liam, as she had been instructed to address him tonight, was quite attractive. He was dressed in black jeans and a black button-down shirt open at the throat. He walked with a limp from a car accident he'd suffered some years back, and he carried a beautiful cane Allie had made for him. Allie, who had hair of an auburn shade Shea would have killed for, wore a toga exactly like hers, except it was a rich, dark red. It matched the red leather collar she wore around her neck.

Beautifully made, the collar had a small gold padlock shaped like a heart at its center.

Not for the first time, Shea wished she had a collar to symbolize her devotion to her Masters and their ownership of her body and soul. She half smiled as she imagined her staid, super-conservative colleagues' reactions if she showed up at the lab in a leather slave collar.

They exchanged greetings and hugs, and Shea led their guests into the living room. She offered them each a glass of the champagne Zach had brought home that afternoon, and Sir Liam, thankfully, assumed the duty of popping the cork. Just as Shea had filled their flutes, the doorbell rang again.

Bonnie and Master Matt stood at the door, Master Taggart and Rylee just behind them. The men, like Sir Liam, were dressed in black, the women wearing the same beautiful red gown as Allie. Bonnie's collar was made from three strands of leather, black, gold and copper, skillfully braided together, while Rylee still had the turquoise collar she had worn since Shea had met her that night at the bonfire.

"They ought to be making a video, especially considering we're all in costume," Rylee quipped as they made their way to the living room.

"Who knows, maybe they will be," Master Taggart replied with a grin.

Master Zach appeared carrying a tray loaded with crackers, cheese and crudités. He took over the duties of pouring the champagne as everyone took seats. Though they had no particular rules in their house about submissives sitting on the furniture, each of their female guests knelt on the rug beside her Dom. Thus, when Zach sat down, Shea knelt likewise on the ground beside him. He put his hand lightly on her shoulder, his touch both comforting and thrilling, as always.

Wonderful smells were wafting from the kitchen, and a moment later, Sir Stephen appeared to greet their guests. Master Zach stood and handed him a glass of champagne.

Like the other Doms, Sir Stephen and Master Zach also wore black. Zach was in his customary thick cotton black T-shirt, leather pants and square-toed boots. Steve, also in leather pants, wore a silk button-down shirt with white mother-of-pearl buttons, characteristically rolled to the forearms.

Sir Stephen held up his glass. "To our lovely birthday girl, and to our good friends."

As Shea blushed scarlet, everyone lifted their glasses and clinked. The champagne was dry and bubbly, and Shea finished her entire glass. After a few minutes of small talk, the oven timer began to ding from the kitchen.

Master Zach rose to his feet. "I'll help you," he said to Sir Stephen.

Sir Stephen nodded as he also stood. "If everyone will move to the dining room, dinner is ready."

There were only five place settings at the long, narrow table, one at each end, two on one side of the table and one on the other side. The table was covered with a crisp, white tablecloth, black linen napkins beside each plate. Large, flat floor cushions had been placed next to each chair, the one in between the two settings obviously for Shea.

Master Matt and Master Taggart took their seats at opposite ends of the table, Sir Liam settling at the single place setting across the table. The subs knelt on cushions beside their Doms.

A moment later, Master Zach and Sir Stephen came in from the kitchen, both carrying platters. Dinner was salad, pork tenderloin and garlic-parmesan green beans. Both red and white wine were offered, along with sparkling water flavored with lemon. It was odd but also somehow extremely erotic to kneel between her Masters, opening her mouth obediently as they took turns placing delicious morsels of food on her tongue. She felt a little silly at first, but then began to enjoy being taken care of in this particular way. She was at once nurtured and controlled, and the combination suited her submissive soul.

When the meal was over, the subs were instructed to remain on their cushions while the Doms cleared the table. The girls whispered and giggled about this being a nice change of events. The guys returned a few moments later, all of them carrying something—a coffee carafe, a tray of mugs and dessert plates and, in Master Zach's hands, a large cake with a ring of lit candles around its edge.

"Girls, stand up and see," Sir Stephen directed as he set down the cake with a flourish. The subs all got to their feet, their eyes on the cake, big smiles on all their faces.

Shea endured the birthday song, willing herself not to blush as she listened to her friends, a few of them woefully off-key. When it was over, Sir Stephen directed her to blow out the candles.

The Doms beckoned their subs to sit on their laps for the dessert course, and Shea settled on Master Zach's knees as Sir Stephen fed her. The cake was her favorite, chocolate mousse with plenty of chocolate buttercream icing, but she barely tasted it. Her stomach filled with butterflies of anticipation for what she knew lay just ahead.

When dessert and coffee were done, Sir Stephen stood and looked down at Shea. "S, from this moment forward and for the duration of the evening, you belong to everyone in this room. You will submit without hesitation to any and everything that is asked of you."

It wasn't a request, but rather a declaration, and his words sent a shiver of fear and desire coursing through Shea's body. "Yes, Sir Stephen," she said softly.

"Girls," Sir Stephen continued, now directing his attention to the women. "Take S to the den and prepare her for presentation. We'll be waiting for you here in the dining room."

The women rose, everyone's eyes on Shea. Rylee came over and placed her hand supportively on Shea's arm and together they walked toward the den. Shea wasn't sure if she felt more like a queen being prepared for her coronation, or a prisoner being led to her execution. Maybe a little of both.

Once in the room, Bonnie turned to Shea. "You doing okay, Shea? Or should I say S?" She smiled.

"That's so cool that they call you S," Allie enthused. "Just like in *Story of O*."

"And you even have your own Sir Stephen," Rylee said.

"I loved when the guards would come in and just whip her and then leave her alone, chained to the wall. Great masturbation material," Allie added.

They all laughed, Shea included.

"Seriously, though," Bonnie said, placing her hand on Shea's arm. "Are you doing okay? Being the center of attention like this can be kind of intimidating, even though it's sexy as hell."

"I'm okay," Shea said, refusing to give in to her nerves. "At least that's what I keep telling myself." She managed a smile.

"We've got our instructions," Rylee said. "Which are to strip, inspect and prepare you for the men."

Rylee reached for one of the clips that held Shea's shoulder straps together. Allie reached for the other. In tandem, they released the clips, and the gown fell open to the waist. Bonnie plucked at the sash and the dress puddled around Shea's feet.

"Have you lost more weight?" Allie asked as she knelt in front of

Shea to remove her sandals.

"Yeah, you better cut it out, or you're going to disappear," Rylee said.

Shea laughed with pleasure. "It's not like I've been dieting or anything. It just kind of melted away." She shrugged. "Oreos and ice cream used to be my best friends."

"I hear you on that one," Rylee said. "They're still pretty darn good friends of mine." She laughed. "If I didn't swim and do Jiu Jitsu all the time, I'd be in serious trouble."

"Focus, girls," Bonnie said, though she was smiling. Addressing herself to Shea, she said, "Stand with your legs shoulder width apart and lock your hands behind your head. I'm going to inspect your body."

Shea was familiar with body inspection. Her Masters required that she keep herself smooth at all times, and occasionally one of them would tell her to assume the inspection position. Though she was careful in her grooming, and certainly more comfortable with her body now, the command always caused her heart to skip a beat. There was something inherently humiliating about being inspected like an animal or a piece of meat. At the same time, the humiliation was oddly thrilling. Thus, while she hated being inspected in this way, she also loved it.

Shea assumed the position, lifting her chin and fixing her focus on the middle distance as she fought down her blush. Bonnie ran her fingers lightly along Shea's underarms, tickling her in the process. A month ago, she would've giggled and jerked away, but now she stood still.

Kneeling, Bonnie ran her hands along Shea's legs. Standing again, she stroked Shea's shaven mons, her fingers sliding between Shea's legs. Her touch sent a jolt of desire directly to Shea's clit, despite the fact she considered herself completely heterosexual.

Allie approached her next, a lipstick in her hands. "Rouged nipples, just like O," she said with a smile. She cupped one of Shea's breasts and ran the lipstick lightly over her areola and rapidly rising nipple. She repeated the process with the second nipple.

Rylee approached, holding something she had retrieved from Steve's desk. She held out a chain leash and leather dog collar. "Lower your arms," Rylee instructed. "We're to lead you to the Masters on this leash."

Shea's heart, which had slowed with the girls' friendly banter, sped up again to a mile a minute as Rylee fastened the dog collar around her throat. When it was on, Bonnie reappeared holding a black satin sleep mask. She placed it over Shea's eyes, careful as she slipped the elastic behind her head.

There was a gentle downward yank on the chain. "On your hands and knees," Rylee said. "You're to crawl."

"The lucky birthday girl," Bonnie said as Shea blindly lowered herself to the ground. There were murmurs of assent.

Shea wasn't sure how lucky she felt at that moment. She could barely hear herself think over the pounding of her heart as the women, flanking her on all sides, led her slowly out of the den and through the living room.

Just inside the dining room door, hands gripped her upper arms, pulling Shea to her feet. There was some rustling and whispers as Shea stood, trying not to fidget, unable to see.

When the blindfold was removed, Sir Stephen stood in front of her, the upper half of his face covered by a black domino mask, only his eyes visible. His dominant gaze pierced her soul.

When he stepped aside, Shea saw that all the men were wearing identical black masks. The effect was at once erotic and chilling, as if she were among strangers—dark and dangerous Masters who would soon have their way with her.

The women, too, wore masks over their eyes, though theirs were of a red that matched their gowns. They were each kneeling on their cushions now, and all eyes were on Shea.

The table had been covered by a new cloth, this one black instead of white, and in front of each Master there was an object. Before Master Taggart lay a small black whip, its tail split at the tip like a snake's tongue. In front of Master Matt was a tall red candle and a box of matches. At Sir Liam's place sat a long riding crop with a looped handle.

Then she saw the cage.

It stood in the corner of the room, moved from its customary place down in the dungeon. She had been in the cage on only two occasions during her training, both brief periods of time-out, but each time she had been thrilled to her bones by the captivity, which sent her to a deeply submissive place the instant the door clanged shut.

Staring now at the tall, narrow cage with its black bars and ceiling just high enough to accommodate a standing adult, she understood the guys had provided a very real prop from the sexual fantasy she'd whispered while masturbating for them in the video it seemed she'd made a lifetime ago.

Without speaking to her, Sir Stephen picked up the end of the leash and led Shea to the cage. He pushed her gently but firmly inside. "Lift your arms high, grip the bars and don't let go until I let you out," he instructed her.

Shea obeyed, taking hold of the cold bars as Sir Stephen removed her leash and collar. He closed the door, leaving her naked and alone in the cage.

Returning to the table, Sir Stephen took his place. Lifting the brandy bottle, he poured a little more into his snifter and then turned to Sir Liam. "I understand your sub has something new to show us."

Sir Liam nodded. "She did the design, I did the piercing. Show them, Allie."

Obediently, Allie stood and reached for the clips at her toga, releasing them one at a time. As the top of her gown fell from her shoulders, Shea could see the small, delicate gold hoops at her nipples. They had been beaded with tiny purple stones Shea thought must be amethyst. The jewelry looked stunning against her small, high breasts, and Shea made a mental note to ask her Masters for nipple rings, even though the thought of needles piercing her flesh frightened her.

Master Taggart went next. "Go on," he instructed Rylee as Allie re-clipped her gown and lowered herself back to her cushion. "Show our friends your latest mark of ownership."

Rylee rose from her cushion and lifted the skirt of her gown to her waist. Without the slightest hesitation or hint of self-consciousness, she spread her labia, revealing three tiny gold rings embedded in the hood of her clit. All of the other girls, including Shea, gasped in awe and admiration while the men grinned at one another.

As Rylee lowered herself back to her cushion, Master Zach said, "What about you guys, Matt? Anything new to show us?"

Master Matt nodded. "Yeah, actually. Something pretty major."

The room became silent, everyone watching and waiting, including Shea, ignored and still clenching the bars of her cage. "We haven't told you guys about this before now, because Bonnie wanted to make sure it healed properly before we showed anyone. We had it done by a pro. We chose the design together, and I'm guessing most of you will recognize what it is."

Murmurs of interest and curiosity rippled through the room as Bonnie stood. She turned so her back was to the table and slowly lifted the skirt of her gown. On her left cheek stood a small but distinct brand, the ridged skin permanently darkened to red.

"It's the BDSM emblem," Sir Stephen said as they all took in the circle with its triple spiral.

"Oh," Shea breathed, recalling her extensive research into all things BDSM in the years before she dared to make it her reality. The symbol was based on a triskele. The triple spirals in a rotating symmetry represented the three divisions of BDSM—B&D, D/s and S&M, and the hole at the center of each spiral symbolized the void within each person who is hardwired for BDSM—a void that can only be filled by a complementary other. BDSM cannot be done alone.

There was excited discussion around the table as several of the guests lightly touched the raised, darkened flesh of her brand, and Master Matt talked about the procedure itself and Bonnie's incredible submissive courage during the ordeal. Shea's ass tingled with sympathy as she tried to imagine the searing heat of the fire-hot brand burning its image permanently into her flesh.

Finally, Bonnie lowered herself back onto her cushion, and all eyes turned toward Shea. Shea, who still held the bars of her cage, gripped them tightly as Master Zach approached her. His eyes behind his mask bored into hers as he unlatched the cage door and pulled it open.

"Drop your hands to your sides," he instructed. As Shea obeyed, he reached for her throat. Gripping her just below the jaw, he pulled her from the cage. Her heart was pounding, his hand on her throat thrusting her instantly into primal sub mode.

He drew her toward the table with his hand. "Bend over and extend your hands out flat on the table," he instructed. "Spread your legs and offer your ass for Master Taggart."

He let her go, and Shea obeyed, resting her cheek against the linen tablecloth, her heart thudding.

Master Taggart came up beside her, the small whip in his large hand. "Thirty strokes for your birthday," Master Taggart announced in his gravelly voice. "And one extra for good luck."

"You will count the strokes out loud," Sir Stephen informed Shea from somewhere behind her.

Shea was reminded of Rylee that night at the bonfire—of how gracefully and stoically she had accepted the Leather Master's single tail, and Shea silently prayed she could do the same tonight.

Master Matt stood on the other side of the narrow table and reached for her wrists, which he pinned to the table with his hands. There was no gentle warm up and no warning as Master Taggart's snake cut across Shea's flesh like the twin blades of a knife. In spite of herself, her first count came out as a yelp.

Her entire ass was soon a crisscross of stinging fire. Despite her prayer, she began to whimper and squirm. By the stroke of twenty, tears were pouring down her cheeks, and by thirty, she was wailing. "Thirty-one," she cried with relief as the last line of fire was drawn across her tortured flesh.

As she lay limp and exhausted, someone tapped her shoulder. Master Zach's voice murmured in her ear, "What are you forgetting, S? Master Taggart gave you a gift."

Shea managed only to lift her head. "Thank you, Master Taggart," she croaked.

"Anytime," he replied with a grin.

Someone smoothed a soothing balm over her ass and thighs. Hands reached for her, helping her to a standing position. Master Zach handed her a glass of water, while Sir Stephen dabbed at her tear-streaked cheeks with a tissue.

"How're you doing?" he asked softly, looking into her eyes from behind his mask.

"I'm good, Sir," she answered, surprised to find this was true. She was better than good. In spite of her stinging flesh, her nudity, her position as the focus of so much attention—or no, because of it all—she was more aroused than she could remember being in her life. She had heard that submissives were natural exhibitionists, but she had never believed it of herself—until now.

Sir Stephen nodded with a knowing smile. "Good. Now, lie on your back on the table. It's time for the next Master to claim you."

The men helped her all the way up onto the table. Because it was so narrow, it barely accommodated her torso, leaving her legs dangling over the side. Someone slipped a cushion beneath her ass, forcing her pelvis upward. Master Zach came up behind her head, supporting it with his thighs so it didn't hang over the other side. Reaching down, he placed the blindfold back over her eyes, plunging her into darkness. Hands pushed her thighs apart, while other hands took hold of her wrists, spreading her on the table in cruciform.

She heard the unmistakable sound of a match striking its box. A moment later, though she had been half-expecting it, a splash of melted wax startled her as it landed on her right breast. It was followed by another drop, and then a series of droplets that fell with burning precision over both nipples. She jerked each time the searing liquid made contact.

As the wax cooled and hardened on her breasts, she was again taken sharply by surprise by the sudden splash of heat against her shaven mons. Hands held her legs open as the wax streamed onto the delicate folds of her pussy. Shea jerked and cried out with each painful splatter.

When the blindfold was finally removed, Shea lifted her head to see the red candle wax hardened in splashed patterns over her breasts and sex, Master Matt still holding the candle, though the flame had been extinguished.

"Thank you, Master Matt," she managed.

He nodded, a smile lifting his lips.

Sir Liam appeared next in front of her, the riding crop in his hand, his mouth lifted in a cruel smile. "We need to remove this wax for the next stage of your birthday celebration," he said. "Nothing like a riding crop to get the job done."

Sir Liam struck her with the small, folded square of leather at the end of the long handle. He tapped at the wax at her breasts and, as it broke into pieces, other men picked and brushed them away.

When the crop smacked against her now extremely tender cunt, it hurt more than the hot wax had, and Shea yelped with pain as she instinctively tried to slam her legs closed, but hands held them apart.

"Courage," Sir Stephen reminded her. "Take what we give you, S. It pleases us to see you suffer, sexy sub girl."

His words settled like a warm cloak over her shivering nerves, and Shea relaxed, breathing deeply as she flowed with the smacking beat of Sir Liam's leather crop. Finally, it was over, and Shea managed to get out her thanks in a trembling voice.

Master Zach now sat in front of her where she lay, splayed and exhausted on the table. On the other side of the narrow table, someone was still supporting her head. Sir Stephen moved to take their place. He stroked her hair back from her face as Master Zach said, "You've suffered well for us. Now we will reward you."

Shea moaned as Master Zach leaned over her and she felt the delicate, wet stroke of his tongue against her tender labia. His hands were on her thighs as he licked and kissed her throbbing sex. Her eyes fluttered shut, but opened when she heard the sound of a zipper. Above her, she saw that Sir Stephen had pulled his thick, erect cock from his pants.

He stepped back so her head now hung off the side of the table. Holding his shaft, he touched the head to her lips, which Shea eagerly parted. As he slid his cock deep into her throat, Shea surrendered to his control, even as her body shuddered with pleasure from Master Zach's skilled mouth and fingers at her sex.

She wanted it to last forever, but the amazing foreplay of the evening, combined with the intense sensory overload of Sir Stephen's cock down her throat and Master Zach's mouth on her cunt, made that impossible. She tried to resist the rising orgasm that was cresting like a wave inside her, but it was already a lost battle. Her entire body was electrified, every nerve ending firing with a fierce, almost painful pleasure.

Sir Stephen's cock fell away from her lips and she began to pant. "Yes, that's it, S," her Master urged. "Come for us. Come for us all."

Gratefully, Shea let go of the last semblance of control and hurtled out over the abyss of pure, blinding, perfect sensation.

When she came back to herself, Shea was cradled in Master Zach's strong, comforting arms. Sir Stephen sat beside them, something in his hands. All the other subs were now in their Masters' laps, and everyone had removed their masks. They were all smiling at her.

"Here's your last present, S," Sir Stephen said as he held out a small gift-wrapped package. We had it specially commissioned just for you."

Commissioned! Shea's eyes flew to the Leather Master. Had her guys had a collar made just for her? Maybe she'd wear it to work anyway—who cared what her boring, vanilla colleagues thought?

She took the gift, her fingers trembling slightly with excitement as she plucked away the ribbon and tore the wrapping from the box. When she lifted the lid, she saw, not a leather collar, but a beautiful necklace made from links of soft, rose gold. "Oh," she breathed as she lifted it from its bed of cotton. "It's beautiful."

"Allie made it," Master Zach said with a grin.

"It's part of my new line of everyday BDSM jewelry for when we're out in the vanilla world," Allie explained with a smile. "Just like the barrette I gave you, it's not necessarily what it appears to be at first glance."

Intrigued, Shea looked more closely at the links of the chain. "They're handcuff links," she exclaimed exultantly. "How cool is that?"

"That's right," Sir Stephen said, taking the chain from her and opening the clasp. "With this collar, Master Zach and I wish to formally claim you for our own. If you allow us to place this necklace around your throat, it's your acceptance of our ownership over your body, heart and soul. And it also symbolizes our commitment to you as your Masters to protect and cherish you within the circle of our love."

As if in a dream, Shea slipped from Master Zach's lap, his arms falling away as she lowered herself to the cushion between them. Kneeling up, she lifted her hair, which had completely escaped its barrette at some point in the evening, and lowered her head to indicate her acceptance.

Sir Stephen placed the necklace around her neck, and Master Zach closed the clasp.

CHAPTER 11

"Picking up your better third today?" Tag asked one afternoon in late November.

Steve laughed. "Yeah. We've been moping around for the past three days without her."

"Oh, better third, better half. I get it," Zach said with a belated smile. It was true—since she left on a business trip for work, they'd hardly known what to do with themselves. Zach had suggested they go down to Hardcore but Steve hadn't wanted to without Shea.

Steve put down his tools and wiped his hands on a rag. "I guess I better get going, in case there's traffic on the way to the airport."

Normally they would have gone together to pick her up, but Tag had asked that one of them stay and help him finish yet another deadline project, and Steve had won the coin toss. The business had really taken off since Rylee had helped the Leather Master establish an online presence. It was only a matter of time before he hired more leather workers.

Steve turned to Zach. "See you at home?"

Zach nodded. "Drive safe."

Tag and he continued to work in companionable silence at their respective worktables for a while. At length, Tag said, "So, how are things going with the three of you?"

"Great," Zach said automatically.

Was it great?

Mostly, yeah, it was pretty great.

Shea had rapidly become an integral part of their lives, even assisting in the training of other subs. She brought a woman's touch, and more especially, a sub's perspective, to the sessions. Beyond that, there was something incredibly sexy about watching their sub girl prepare another woman for a scene—helping her strip, assume the proper positions, and even assisting in the actual training from time to time.

Zach had never regretted collaring Shea that night at her birthday party. He had settled happily into a full-time role as Shea's Master and lover, and the deep friendship he shared with Steve hadn't been eroded by their new living arrangement, as he had feared it might.

He had been a little worried, especially at first, that he would lose his autonomy, his very sense of self, once a girlfriend had been formally introduced in their midst, but things had worked out surprisingly well. They each had their own space, and, while more often than not the three of them ended up in Steve's much larger master bedroom at night, from time to time Zach stayed in his own room, and Shea stayed in hers.

Yet sometimes, especially on occasional times when the three of them had gone to sleep in their own beds but Zach had found Shea had slipped at some point in the night into Steve's room, Zach had to admit he got a little jealous. At those times, he was reminded of why he had always avoided romantic relationships in the first place.

He hated those feelings of jealousy in himself, which he saw as a weakness. He was better than that, he would tell himself when the green-eyed monster reared its ugly head. Shea and Steve deserved better.

Zach realized Tag was staring at him in that brooding way he had, his head cocked slightly to one side. "Great, but..." Tag said, a quizzical smile on his face.

"What?" Zach said defensively, hunching his shoulders and looking away. What was the guy, a mind reader?

"Nothing. It's just that I know what a hard time I had getting my head around a relationship with *one* person, much less two. I can only imagine the complications of a ménage. I mean"—he shrugged—"I would think sometimes one of you might feel like the odd guy out."

"Ha," Zach said, the word bursting from his mouth like a punch. "It's funny you say that. I mean, don't get me wrong, things really are terrific between the three of us. And yeah, I'm the guy who always thought of *relationship* as a four-letter word, but somehow this thing really is working out great." He looked away from Tag, suddenly embarrassed by the other man's apparent scrutiny.

"But..." Tag persisted.

"Okay, yeah," Zach admitted, no longer meeting Tag's gaze. "Sometimes I think Shea and Steve might have more of an intense connection than I can manage, but that's just because I'm such a relationship-phobe. They're both really good about giving me space when I need it. It's a terrific setup."

He was talking too fast, trying too hard to convince, but still he barreled on. "I figured out what's different with Shea, compared to the other women I've been with. With past lovers, it was about getting my own satisfaction. I mean, I made sure they got what they needed, but in the end it was really about me."

He flashed a look at Tag, who nodded. "I hear you on that one."

"It's like I had my life all split up into different parts. Lovers in one box, and then our trainees in another. That way I got to really let my need to dominate and control exert itself without worrying about all the responsibilities that go with being someone's Dom. But with Shea, it's been different. With Shea, with the three of us together, something has just kind of clicked, you know?"

"I do know," Tag said. "I've seen the three of you together, don't forget. It's like she's the missing piece. The only reason I'm pressing is because I've been there and done that in the screw-up-relationships department, and I nearly lost Rylee in the process."

Zach was quiet for a long moment as he worked a leather sheath over the whip handle he had been honing. And yet...there it was, lurking just beneath the surface. In his heart of hearts, if he was brutally honest, Zach was afraid that the bond between Shea and Steve was stronger than what he himself was capable of. They knew how to trust on a deeper level, and it was that connection, more than anything, which he both longed for and feared.

What was his problem? Everything was fine. Just fine.

He looked up at Tag with a bright smile. "Nah," he said. "Everything's great."

Later that evening as they packed up their work tools, Taggart said, "I'm taking Rylee to Hardcore after we grab a quick bite. Maybe we'll see you guys there."

"Yeah, maybe," Zach said noncommittally. "I'll see what Steve and Shea think."

It was nearly eight o'clock by the time Zach got on the road. Barring horrible traffic, Steve would have probably beaten him home, but only just. Zach was excited to see Shea. Maybe they'd take her right down to the dungeon and put her through her paces, in case she had gotten rusty during her absence.

He could already envision her naked and on her knees, her face upturned, her mouth open for his cock. He could imagine her suspended by her wrists, her arms spread wide over her head, her toes barely touching the ground. They would move in slow circles around her body, taking turns snapping their whips against her soft, supple skin. Steve would focus on her ass, while Zach lashed her luscious breasts with a single tail.

Allie had just finished the nipple rings they'd commissioned, and they waited at home in a small, velvet box. Though Zach didn't usually care much about jewelry, he had to admit these were really special—a pair of silver barbells, each with a delicate hanging chain on which was balanced a tiny ruby heart. They planned to give them to Shea that night to keep by her bedside until she was ready for her piercing.

How ironic that Steve, the decidedly more sadistic of the two of them, had asked Zach to do the honors. Though Steve had no trouble whipping girls until they cried, or binding them in painful positions and subjecting them to intense erotic torture until they were begging for mercy, when it came to needles, the guy was a total wimp.

Zach smiled indulgently at the thought of his friend's squeamishness. The sight of blood never bothered Zach. Not that he planned to draw any blood, beyond a possible unavoidable drop at the piercing site. He had experience with body piercing, and had even tried his hand at it professionally for a while back in his early twenties when he was still finding his way.

He smiled as he drove, recalling Shea's near-obsession regarding the piercing the week before she'd left for her business trip as she ping-ponged between excitement and fear. He'd observed that particularly submissive reaction before.

So much of BDSM was the sensual mind-fuck—letting the sub know what was going to happen to them later that hour, or day, or even week. Initial resistance or even outright refusal would slowly edge its way into a, "Maybe I can do that for my Master, but it won't really be for me."

A good Master would give his sub the time she needed to come around. He'd planted the seed, and now he'd add water and sunlight. He would talk about the process, the procedure, and how it would please him, as well as satisfy her submissive needs, but he wouldn't press, not too hard.

She would begin to shift in her mind, waging her own internal battle. "He wants it, and yeah, it would be pretty hot. But can I really handle it? Will it hurt too much? What if I fail? What if I have to use my safeword?"

This would slowly edge into, "Okay, he wants this for me, and he believes in me. He says I can handle this, and so I can. I will do this to please my Master."

Without her realizing it, the anticipation would begin to get the upper hand over the fear. She would start to think about it constantly. She would research it online, and talk with other subs who had undergone the same experience. It would take over her thoughts, whether she was at work, or bound in the dungeon, or beneath her lover's body as he fucked her. After a while, she would no longer just be accepting of what her Master wanted. She would crave it—she would beg for it, not just to please him, but to quench the burning fire now raging in her submissive soul.

Then, and only then, was she truly ready to submit.

The garage door was open, and Zach pulled in alongside Steve's car, cut the engine and climbed out, excited to see their sub girl after so many days apart. He opened the door to the house and entered the kitchen. No one was there.

"Hello?" he called as he made his way toward the living room.

Then he saw them.

Steve had Shea pinned against the wall by her wrists. His head was lowered to hers and it was clear they were kissing. Her suitcase and purse were on the floor beside them, the suitcase on its side as if it had been flung there in their haste to get at each other.

As Zach stood, frozen in place, Steve let go of Shea's arms, which she wrapped around his neck, pulling him closer. He reached beneath her, lifting her into his arms as her legs came up around his waist. Through it all, they remained locked in a passionate kiss.

The kiss went on and on, as if the pair were long-lost lovers, as if nothing else—no one else—mattered, or ever had mattered.

"Fuck," Zach whispered. The jealousy he'd managed to keep tamped down for so long suddenly opened its slobbering, gaping jaws and sank its sharp teeth into Zach's heart.

Tag was right—two was hard enough, but three? Yes, he'd sworn to cherish and protect Shea, but she already had one Master, the one who held her now in his arms. She didn't need two. Neither of them needed him. He was superfluous, an extra, the third wheel.

Silently, he backed out of the room, his keys still in his hand. He opened the door to the garage, hesitating a moment on the threshold. He could turn around and call out in a loud voice that he was home, and then pretend everything was hunky dory.

Or he could leave.

After all, it wasn't as if the three of them were joined at the hip.

Steve had every right to kiss Shea.

And Zach had every right to go out on his own. He didn't need anyone's permission.

He climbed back into his car and turned the key. It had been too long. Hardcore was calling his name.

The underground space was bathed in an eerie, red glow, the odor of sweat, perfume and desire heavy in the air. Several of the scene stations were already occupied by leather-clad Doms and nearly naked subs. Whips cracked, women moaned, men grunted. Zach turned to glance reflexively toward Steve, to reach for Shea, but he was alone.

He wasn't dressed for the scene, still in his work shirt and jeans, the scent of leather oil on his fingers. He had no gear bag and no particular agenda, except to be away from the house where Steve and Shea were probably at this very moment making love.

"Hey there, stranger. Long time no see. I was hoping I'd get lucky tonight."

Zach looked down to see Megan Landry, a one-time casual lover he used to play with in the scene. "Oh, hey there, Megan. I didn't know you were back in Portland."

They embraced. She still looked good—blond, petite and slender, dressed for the night in a red leather mini skirt and matching vest that barely covered her small, high breasts, very tall stiletto heels on her feet. Her only flaw was pockmarked skin, ravaged from teenage acne, but mostly covered by the heavy makeup she wore at all times, even in bed.

"Just for the week visiting family. I can take them for about twenty-four hours before I remember why I moved to California. I was barely off the plane before my mom reminded me I wasn't getting any younger and started demanding to know when I planned to get married and give her grandbabies. Then there's my annoying, live-in-the-basement-and-sponge-off-mom-and-dad-forever brother with his million reasons why the world is out to get him. I had to get out of there before I went postal on someone."

Zach laughed. He'd forgotten how funny Megan could be. He glanced around the club and then looked back at Megan. "I don't have any of my gear with me, but if you wanted to do a scene, maybe…?"

Even as he said it, a small barb of guilt pierced his gut.

Then the memory of that kiss—that passionate, excluding kiss—resurfaced from where it had been lurking in his mind, and he yanked the barb free and tossed it aside. He was his own man. He could do whatever the fuck he wanted.

"We can borrow something from the club rack," Megan said. "I could really use a good, cleansing whipping after the year, uh, I mean the week I've spent at my parents'."

They moved together toward the whip rack the club provided for people who didn't bring their own gear. "Aw," Megan said in a whining tone. "No canes left. No single tails. Shit." She chose a red flogger with a long, fat handle and handed it to Zach. The handle was poorly balanced, the throws made of cheap, hard leather, but it was better than nothing.

Megan led him toward a free station near the entrance of the club. The station contained a St. Andrew's cross with cuffs attached, the wood rubbed smooth from usage and darkened with sweat. As always happened for any public scene at Hardcore, people began to gather along the edges of the station mat to watch the action. Most of them were single men with that hungry, slack-jawed look they probably wore when they were home alone at their computers, searching for free porn to jack off to.

Ignoring them, Zach watched as Megan unzipped her mini skirt and edged it down her slender legs. She wore a thong beneath it, and her lower back and ass were covered in ink. At first glance, it was just a mass of red, black and blue, but as he stared at it, he saw it was an elaborate tattoo of blue roses entwined with thorn-covered vines, droplets of bright red blood dripping from each thorn.

"Whoa," Zach said, "that's a lot of ink. When did you get that?"

"My Dom is a tattoo artist," Megan said with evident pride as she craned her head to regard her small ass. "He's going to cover my entire body with ink. I get a real rush from the pain. Isn't it fucking amazing?"

"Uh, yeah. Really great," Zach managed, though in fact he found it way overdone.

Megan took off her vest and stepped up to the cross, lifting her arms so Zach could buckle her into the wrist cuffs. He set the flogger down on the mat. She spread her legs as Zach crouched behind her to cuff her ankles into place. She wore a strong perfume, something spicy that tickled his nose. Zach suddenly missed Shea's subtle vanilla scent with an ache that actually made him catch his breath. What was he doing there?

Giving them space.

After all, he was the one who had resisted the romance, who claimed he didn't want to be tied down, who liked to keep his options open…

He stood and picked up the crappy flogger. The men crowding him shuffled back a little as he took up his position behind Megan. He thought about Shea that first night they'd seen her sitting on the sofa, leaning forward with such yearning on her face, such longing…

Before he realized what he was doing, he turned back to that same sofa, as if Shea might be there now, watching him with those lovely, gold-rimmed blue eyes.

Instead, a couple was making out on one end of the couch, the woman perched on the man's lap, both of them stuffed into cheap-looking leather outfits several sizes too small. On the other end, two guys were leaning in to one another, their thighs touching, their hands on each other's crotches.

"I'm ready, babe," Megan called out. "Any time this week would be good."

He turned back to the cross. "Oh, sorry."

You should be with Shea and Steve, not here with this woman you used to know, surrounded by strangers. What are you doing here? Go home.

"What's your safeword?" he asked automatically.

"You don't remember? I'm crushed," she replied in a teasing tone.

"Uh…" Zach tried to recall what it might be, but only Shea's funny, fancy chemistry term came to mind—*zirconium.*

"It's rosebud," Megan supplied. "Not that I'll need it with that shitty little flogger. You know I like it rough. The harder the better."

He swished the cheap leather tresses over Megan's ass and back, trying to get into a rhythm. His phone buzzed in his pocket. Maybe they were done fucking now and had finally realized he hadn't come home yet.

He hit Megan harder, whipping the leather tresses in a stinging arc over her back and shoulders. She moaned her approval. "More, baby," she urged. "More, more, more."

He struck her with force, putting his muscle into it so her body was pushed hard against the cross. The tresses left long, red marks along her narrow back. She yelped but then thrust her ass out, the invitation clear.

The men swayed and murmured behind him, their presence

unwelcome. He turned briefly to glare at them, and they took a collective step back, their eyes fixed on the bound, nearly naked girl, their hands hovering on or near their crotches.

Blocking them out as best he could, Zach whipped Megan's thin little body, covering her ass, back and thighs with a whirlwind of flying red leather. If he just focused on the scene, on giving this girl what she needed, on letting the process clear his mind, he could deal with whatever it was that was tearing at his gut. He could keep his own pain at bay.

It didn't work.

As vividly as if they were standing in front of him, Zach saw Shea's arms circling Steve's neck as Steve lifted her into his arms.

"Do it, baby. Take me all the way," Megan cried in a hoarse voice as she gyrated her pelvis against the wooden cross.

Zach bit down hard on his lower lip to keep from shouting as the sharp memory of Steve and Shea locked in their lovers' embrace, kissing with a passion from which he was excluded looped around and around in his head, tightening with each repetition like a noose around his heart.

What a jerk I've been to think this relationship thing could possibly work. What the hell was I thinking all this time? I'm not cut out for this shit. Better they should be alone.

"Rosebud, rosebud, rosebud!"

The repeated word finally penetrated the fog of his misery at the same moment a large, heavy hand clamped his shoulder. "Dude, I think that's her safeword."

Zach whipped his head in the direction of the deep, gravelly voice he knew so well. Taggart Fitzgerald stood beside him, his hand still on Zach's shoulder.

Shock ricocheted through Zach's body. He dropped the flogger as if it were on fire. "Oh, shit," he breathed, appalled that he'd made Megan use her safeword. "Fuck."

Megan's back was a deep crimson red, her tattooed ass mottled with bruises that were already forming, welts visible on the backs of her thighs. She was whimpering, her hands clenched into fists, her entire body shaking.

Zach leaped forward and jerked away the Velcro bindings on her wrists and ankles. As she fell back, he turned the shaking girl gently toward him and pulled her into a light embrace, careful not to hurt her any more than he already had. "I'm so sorry, Megan," he said into her hair. "I'm so sorry. I didn't mean to go that far."

Pulling back, she looked up at him. Tear tracks ran through her thick makeup, smudges of mascara beneath her eyes, her lipstick smeared over the cheek that had been resting against the wood. But instead of the angry reproach he expected and deserved, her mouth lifted into a broad grin. "No apologies necessary, babe," she said breathlessly. "That was the *best* beating I've had in months. I don't know why I wimped out at the end." She stood on tiptoe and kissed his mouth. "Let's do it again!"

"I think you've had enough, young lady," Taggart said, stepping forward as the hangers-on wandered away to find more action. He turned to Zach. "You okay, man? Steve texted me a while back asking if you were still at work. I texted you, too. You aren't answering anyone's texts. What's going on?"

"Who is this gorgeous hunk of pure, raw manhood?" Megan chirped, inserting herself between the two of them. She cupped her bare breasts and winked at Tag. "I still have one side that needs heating."

"This is the Leather Master," a low, feminine voice Zach recognized as Rylee Miller, replied, appearing just beside her man and placing her hand on his arm in a gesture that clearly said *He's mine.* "You okay?" she said, flashing Zach a worried gaze.

He shrugged. "Sure." Though he wasn't. He'd just ignored someone's safeword. That had never, ever happened to him before.

"Oh," Megan said, fixing Rylee with a sharp, appraising gaze and then taking a step back. "I see." She gave a small shrug, as if acknowledging defeat. "I'm Megan Landry. An old friend of Zach's."

"Looks like you could use some aftercare," Taggart said to Megan as he looked her over. He dipped his head so his mouth was close to Rylee's ear and murmured something, then, adding in a louder voice, "Rylee, sweetheart, could you take care of Megan while Zach and I talk a minute?"

"Sure," Rylee replied, giving Zach another concerned look before turning to Megan. "If that works for you, Megan?"

Megan gave Tag a last, lingering gaze, and then shrugged and nodded. "Thanks, Zach. I'm going to have some yummy bruises to make my guy jealous." She bent and retrieved her clothing.

As the two girls walked toward one of the aftercare stations, Taggart led Zach to a table in the bar area. "Sit down. I'll get you some water."

Zach, still dazed, sat as Taggart went to the bar. He returned a moment later with a cold bottle. Zach accepted it, twisted off the cap and drank the whole thing down in one long gulp.

Tag put his hand on Zach's arm. "What's going on, Zach? Why are you here alone, especially on the night Shea's coming home? How come they don't know where you are?"

"Because I lied, okay?" Zach spat bitterly. "When you asked how everything is going and I said great, I was lying to us both. I've been feeling weird lately about this whole ménage thing, about this whole relationship thing, but I've been pushing it down, trying to tell myself it's all okay, and everything's great."

Zach pressed his lips together to keep from saying too much. Surely Tag didn't want to hear all this.

"But..." Tag finally urged. "It's not great? What happened?"

"That third wheel thing, that's what happened," Zach blurted. "You said it yourself earlier today, and I tried to pretend it wasn't an issue. Then I got home and saw the two of them."

Tag shook his head. "I'm not following. What do you mean you saw the two of them? Of course, you saw them—they live there. Steve went to fetch Shea at the airport."

"I saw them kissing."

Tag continued to look puzzled.

"Not just kissing," Zach elaborated. "I mean, they were *really* kissing, like in the movies, you know? Like they were madly, crazy in love. I've never kissed Shea like that. Shit, I've barely kissed her at all. I don't really *do* kissing, you know? I mean it's so...it's so..." He struggled for the word.

"Intimate?" Tag suggested.

"Yeah," Zach agreed.

Why *hadn't* he kissed Shea more often? And if he really didn't want to be in a relationship, why had seeing the two of them locked together torn something loose inside him?

"You should text them or call, Zach. Let them know you're okay."

Zach shook his head, a fresh wave of anguished self-pity assailing him. "I doubt they even know I'm not there. That's how into each other they were. They're probably both asleep after their great sex, all wrapped up in each other's arms."

Tag shook his head slowly and then, to Zach's astonishment, began to laugh.

"What?" Zach demanded. "What the fuck's funny about that? About any of this?"

Still laughing, Tag said, "Remember when I said I nearly lost Rylee?"

"Yeah," Zach said, still not getting what Tag thought was so hilarious about his life falling down around his ears.

"I had issues. I honestly believed I was broken, damaged goods, and that I had to let Rylee go. I was giving her the sob speech about how fucked up I was and how it would never work, and you know what she said to me?"

"What?" Zach said, forgetting his own problems for a moment. Tag, normally pretty reserved, had never shared anything so personal with him before.

Still grinning, Tag said, "My sweet, submissive girlfriend put her hands on her hips and said that was the stupidest thing she'd ever heard. She basically told me to get over it. To be a man and face what might be the scariest thing people like you and me have to deal with."

"Which is...?"

"Feelings, Zach. It's scary to have real feelings for someone. I haven't known you all that long, but I knew you before you met Shea and I know you now, and you've become a different person, both you and Steve have. It's like she was the spark, the thing that brought you both to life. Don't fuck that up, Zach, just because you saw them kissing after they'd been apart for a few days."

Tag leaned forward, speaking earnestly. "Look, I get it—it's a huge risk to take, the risk that you might love someone who doesn't love you back, or doesn't love you precisely the way you think they should. It's got to be even tougher when it's three instead of just two, but that doesn't mean it's not worth fighting for. Trust me, Zach, if you can get past that fear, there's a whole wonderful world waiting for you. Waiting at home with Steve and Shea; waiting for you, if you can find the courage to reach for it."

The sweet, welcome scent of vanilla wafted suddenly beneath Zach's nose as Tag leaned back and smiled, his gaze fixed just past Zach's shoulder. A moment later, Steve said from behind him, "There you are, Zach. Why didn't you answer your texts? You had us worried sick."

"Thank goodness Rylee texted me," Shea said, appearing now in his line of vision, her pretty face a mask of concern. "We were about to start calling the hospital emergency rooms."

Zach pushed back from his chair and stood, turning to face the two people he cared most about in the world. Without another word, they enfolded him in their arms.

Chapter 12

"We missed you," Shea said as they released each other. She searched Zach's face with worried eyes. "You gave us a scare."

"I'm sorry," Zach said, and he meant it. It was as if he'd just awakened from a nightmare. He felt disoriented but glad to be back.

Rylee had returned and stood beside Tag at the table.

"Is Megan okay?" Zach asked, ashamed of how he'd bungled the scene, of how he'd used Megan to escape his own pain.

"She's fine," Rylee said with a grin. "She's already found someone else to scene with at the wax station."

Tag got to his feet and put his arm around Rylee. "We'll leave you three to it. I'm sure Zach has some stuff he needs to say." He looked meaningfully at Zach.

Zach nodded as he tried to harness and control the jumble of feelings knocking around inside him. He managed to smile as he said, "Thanks, guys, for having my back. I'm not sure what the fuck I was doing."

"Nobody ever said this relationship stuff was easy," Rylee said with a kind smile.

"But it's definitely worth it," Tag added.

After the couple drifted away to enjoy a scene of their own, the three of them sat at the table. Shea was the first to speak. "What happened, Zach? What made you run away like that?"

Zach glanced from Shea to Steve, his heart twisting at the memory of their passionate kiss. A part of him wanted to lie—to say he didn't know—but it had to be faced. He couldn't pretend he hadn't seen what he'd seen. Girding himself, he blurted, "When I came home tonight, I saw you guys kissing. I know you're in love with each other."

To his shock, Shea smiled, while Steve actually chuckled and said, "Well, duh."

"So, you admit it," Zach said breathlessly, his heart contracting painfully in his chest.

"Of course we admit it, you dope," Steve said, the laugh still in his voice.

Shea said, "We didn't realize you were there, Zach."

"Obviously," he retorted, unable to hide the bitterness from his voice.

"No, you misunderstand me, I think," she said, taking his hand. "If we'd known you were home, I would have jumped on you next." She squeezed his hand as she ducked her head, a trace of a blush moving over her cheeks. "What I'm trying to say—what both Steve and I are trying to say is, yeah, we're in love. But the really great thing is I'm in love with *you*, too."

"That's what's so fucking awesome about our relationship, Zach," Steve said earnestly. "We both love the same girl. We've both claimed the same sub. You and I are best friends—closer than brothers—and somehow we've found a way to make this work."

Zach looked from Steve to Shea, the image of Shea wrapped around Steve still burning in his mind. "Really?" he said hopefully, desperately wanting it to be so. "You love me, too, Shea? As much as you love Steve?"

She nodded. "With all my heart. I love you both."

"This is new for all of us. We just have to trust the process, Zach," Steve added, placing his hand on Zach's shoulder. "We couldn't have this amazing connection without you, Zach. It's not just about Shea and me, or Shea and you. It's all three of us. That's what makes this relationship work. That's what makes it so special. You're a part of us. Without you, the circle would be incomplete. It would just be a straight line between two."

"Now," Shea said, getting to her feet. "It's been a really long day and I'm beat. Let's go home."

Back at their place, Zach went to his own bathroom to wash up. He stripped down to his boxers and walked down the hall to Steve's room. When he stuck his head in the doorway, he saw that Shea was already in Steve's bed, Steve still in the bathroom.

Zach approached the bed, unsure of himself, unsure of her. She flashed him a radiant, dimpled smile and, in spite of himself, he smiled back. "Take off those boxers," she commanded. "I need to feel your body next to mine."

With a grin, Zach pulled off his shorts and sat on the bed, pulling Shea into an embrace. He started to lie down beside her, but she patted the mattress on her other side. "Lie here tonight, between us."

When Zach hesitated, she added softly, "Zach, when you didn't come home tonight, Steve and I both felt as if we were missing a piece of our hearts. Don't do that again, okay? Don't leave us like that."

"No," he promised. "I won't." He lay down in the middle of the bed and Shea snuggled up against him, her sweet warmth soothing his soul.

She reached for his face and brushed his lips with hers. She kissed him lightly as she pressed her body against his. "I love you, Master Zach. I'm so glad you're home where you belong."

She pulled him closer, her arms encircling his neck as her tongue slipped into his mouth, and Zach abandoned himself to her passionate kiss. As they embraced, all the worries, insecurities and fears slid away like an old skin he no longer needed, and which no longer served him.

When they finally released each other, Zach felt a hand on his back and realized Steve had joined them in the bed. "Welcome home, bro," Steve said quietly. "Now our circle is complete."

"Yes," Zach agreed with a happy laugh. He felt lighter than air, anchored only by the loving touch of his best friends on either side of him. "I think I finally get it. You two are the *we* of me."

~*~

It was Steve's turn, and as he took his seat in the tattoo artist's chair, his heart began to race. His jaw was clenched so tight that it hurt. He was being ridiculous. Both Shea and Zach had undergone the process barely batting an eye, even as tiny drops of blood beaded beneath the relentless pierce of the inked tattoo needle.

The tattoo had been Zach's idea—a symbol, he'd said, of their commitment to each other. He'd first brought it up nearly a month ago, just after his misguided solo venture to Hardcore. At first Steve had dismissed it out of hand, but over time, especially given both Zach's and Shea's enthusiasm for the project, he'd come around.

Shea had come up with the idea of the BDSM emblem, the triple spiral based on a triskele that symbolized the three aspects of BDSM. "Except in our case, there's an added meaning," she'd noted, "since the circle of our special relationship contains three."

Steve loved the idea in theory. If only there hadn't been needles involved.

As a tattoo artist swabbed the skin on Steve's inner arm, Shea took a seat on the chair on his other side and took Steve's free hand in hers.

Zach, just behind him, placed a comforting hand on his shoulder and gave it a gentle squeeze. "Relax, bro," he said. "Take the advice that we give our trainees. Embrace the pain and flow with it. Find the courage to submit."

Steve nodded, drew in a deep breath and released it slowly.

"All good?" the tattoo artist inquired.

"As good as it's going to get," Steve said, attempting to laugh.

The tattoo needle buzzed like a dentist's drill as it pricked the sensitive skin on Steve's inner arm again and again and again. It hurt like hell, and without a single masochistic bone in his body, Steve wasn't able to find any pleasure in the process. Instead, sweat breaking out on his forehead and upper lip, he powered his way through it.

"You're doing great," Shea said, and Steve realized he was holding her hand so hard that he was probably hurting her. He made an effort to ease his grip and somehow managed to smile back.

Mercifully, the tattoo artist was skilled and quick, and the quarter-sized emblem was done in twenty minutes.

Steve leaned back in the reclining chair with a sigh of relief as the needle ceased its demonic buzz. Happiness began to bloom in his chest like strong liquor as Shea and Zach both held out their arms to compare the three identical tattoos. The euphoria he experienced went beyond the release of endorphins caused by the pain, or from relief that it was over.

As his two best friends smiled down at him, he understood his happiness stemmed from the simple but profound joy of loving and being loved.

~*~

Shea lay naked on the bondage table, the small box of jewelry balanced on her flat stomach. Her nipples, dark pink gum drops in the centers of her creamy, soft breasts, beckoned to Zach. Her eyes were wide with anticipation, nervous energy radiating from her like an aura.

Steve stood at the head of the table, his hands resting lightly on Shea's arms. His shoulders were hunched, his lips pressed into a thin line.

"Take a deep breath and let it out slowly," Zach counseled, speaking as much to Steve as to Shea. He set down his piercing kit on the small, portable table he'd placed nearby, along with the large hand mirror so he could show Shea afterward.

He focused on the girl, a thrill of power surging through his loins as he held up the piercing needle. "It's not too late to change your mind, S," he said. "Do you still want this?"

"More than anything, Sir," she breathed, some of the tension leaving her body.

Zach looked at Steve, wondering how to calm down his friend, who had turned slightly green at the sight of the needle. "And you, Sir Stephen. Remind us all why we're piercing our sub girl's nipples today."

As he had hoped, Steve seemed to rally at this invitation to be a more direct part of the process. Steve smiled down at Shea as he stroked the tattoo on her inner arm, identical to Zach's and his, that they'd gotten two weeks before. "All three of us share a tattoo, a mark of our commitment to each other, but only you will be pierced today, S." Steve moved his hand from her arm to the necklace they had given her. "While this collar is a symbol of your constant submission to Master Zach and me, the nipple piercing symbolizes an even deeper D/s commitment."

Zach smiled to himself, pleased to realize his old kneejerk resistance to anything approaching permanence of commitment had completely fallen away. Gone, too, was the jealousy at the love between Steve and Shea, the closeness he had once wrongly believed he was incapable of sharing. Though Shea, as their submissive, was the natural focal point of the relationship, it truly was a circle, each of the three of them an integral, necessary part of the whole.

As Steve talked, Zach unwrapped two cannula needles and set them at the ready on the tray. Confidence had returned to Steve's voice as he spoke, his natural dominance reemerging. "Though hidden from the vanilla world, these ruby hearts will be a constant, secret reminder that you belong to us. This permanent mark of ownership is an honor that you have earned, sweet girl, and one we are, in turn, honored to bestow."

Zach tore open a Betadine pad and swabbed Shea's right nipple, which instantly stiffened to his touch. He took one of the pieces of nipple jewelry from the open box still balanced on Shea's belly. Removing the small ruby heart, he threaded the stud to the end of the piercing needle. Gripping Shea's nipple, he pulled it taut.

She stiffened, catching her breath. Zach glanced at Steve, who understood. He stroked Shea's cheek and said, "Breathe deeply and slowly, S. Remember, flow with the pain. Accept it as our gift to you."

"Yes, Sir Stephen. Thank you, Sir." Shea's voice was calm, her body relaxed. She was ready.

"Stay very still," Zach said, fully focused now on what he was doing. "You'll feel a pinch and some heat. Just a few seconds."

He pushed the needle through the soft, spongy flesh of her nipple, pulling the threaded stud through the tiny hole. Shea yipped, but remained still, and in a moment, it was done. A tiny bead of blood appeared in the wake of the needle, which he quickly dabbed away before reattaching the ruby heart.

He placed his hand on Shea's heart, which pounded against his palm. "You did great," he said, beaming down at her.

"It's done, Sir?" Shea said, lifting her head to see. "That was so fast."

"It's done," Zach said, "and it's beautiful, right, Sir Stephen?"

Some of the greenish tinge had returned to Steve's face, but he managed to smile as he agreed, "It's absolutely gorgeous."

The second one was completed just as quickly, without even a single drop of blood. "Want to see?" he asked Shea, who nodded eagerly. He picked up the hand mirror as Steve helped Shea into a sitting position on the table, cradling her from behind.

"Oooh," Shea breathed, her face glowing with submissive radiance as she stared into the mirror at the ruby hearts at her nipples. "They're perfect. Two hearts from my two Masters."

~*~

Six Months Later

"Good job, O'Connor." Shea's boss slapped her on the back. They stood together in the hall just outside the conference room of their newest prospective client's corporate office in Seattle. "Your presentation was excellent. I'm pretty sure I'll be able to clinch the deal over dinner. Sorry I can't bring you along," he added insincerely. "You know, with the budget cuts and all..." He shrugged helplessly, though she knew he was full of shit.

Whenever their client rep was female and even remotely

attractive, Mr. Carroll found a way to exclude Shea from any social activity. Ms. Baxter, a very attractive forty-something woman with no evidence of a wedding ring was right up his horn-dog alley. Hopefully he wouldn't queer the deal in the process of his attempted seduction.

Meanwhile, Shea vastly preferred returning alone to her hotel room. She would order room service and then check in with her Masters. "No worries, Mr. Carroll," she said with a smile as insincere as his. "Wrapping up the deal is your strong suit. I'm just happy to be a part of the process."

"That's the team spirit, O'Connor," he said heartily, again slapping her on the back. "We'll get an early start back to the office in the morning."

Feeling pleased with how she'd handled herself, Shea stepped out into the summer sunshine and took a cab from the client's office to the hotel. It was hard to believe nearly a year had passed since she had met her Masters. Though she had only left them that morning, she already missed Steve and Zach a ridiculous amount, and couldn't wait to have a little FaceTime with them. Maybe they'd want her to strip and masturbate for them, something they often had her do when she had to be away on business.

Her clit pulsed, her pierced nipples tingling at the thought. She had to resist the sudden urge to slip her hands into her bra to fondle the beautiful rings Zach had placed there. The tattoos they'd gotten had been nothing compared to the pain the piercing had caused, but it had been worth every second.

It had been a reversal of their usual roles—with Sir Stephen offering incredible support and love as he helped her through the process, while Master Zach had been masterful in his role as sensual sadist. Between the two of them, in spite of her fear, they'd managed to make the process deeply erotic and enormously satisfying.

How far she had come from the awkward, painfully shy girl who had laid herself over Sir Stephen's lap at the club, her heart nearly pounding out of her chest. How wonderful it was to submit to two men who loved and cherished her. How amazing to feel fully actualized and content with herself in all aspects of her life.

The cab pulled up in front of the hotel. Shea paid the driver and entered the hotel lobby. As she waited for the elevator, she took off her tailored suit jacket and draped it over her arm.

A handsome older man with silver hair and dark eyes entered the elevator along with her. He smiled appreciatively at her, his gaze sweeping her body before returning to her face. She smiled back, thinking how, just a year ago, she would have blushed beet red at his attentions.

The elevator door opened at her floor, and she stepped out, fishing in her bag for her key card as she walked to her room. She inserted the card into the slot and, just as she opened the door, someone grabbed her from behind, placing one arm against her throat as he pushed her forward into the room.

Startled and terrified, she tried to scream, but her cry was muffled by a large hand clamped hard over her mouth. As she struggled in her assailant's grip, something was placed over her eyes, plunging her into darkness.

Her heart was smashing in her chest and her legs felt like rubber as she was half pushed, half carried through the room. She was thrown down hard against the mattress, the man behind her falling on top of her, his heavy weight pinning her down, his hand still clamped hard on her mouth.

When he took his hand from her mouth, Shea again tried to scream, but this time a rubber ball was shoved between her teeth. The man was still holding her down and, she realized as the ball gag strap was buckled around the back of her head, that there must be two men in the room with her. Her heart was pounding so hard she thought she might faint.

Still holding her tight, the man on top of her rolled to his back, pulling her with him so she now lay face up on top of him, blindfolded and gagged. He held her arms while a second pair of hands ripped at her blouse in a spray of buttons. Something cold and hard slipped between her breasts, just beneath her bra. As it was yanked upward in a tear of fabric, she understood it was a knife and her blood turned to ice in her veins.

Her skirt was torn from her body, her pantyhose and panties pulled down her legs. Rough hands kneaded her breasts, tugging lightly at her nipple rings as she squirmed, her panic rising.

The man beneath her shifted, sliding away so she now lay flat on her back on the mattress. She lay helpless, naked, blindfolded and gagged—at the mercy of two men she couldn't see.

The man holding her arms now grabbed her wrists and, pressing them together, drew them over her head, while at the same time her thighs were forcibly parted.

As she bucked and struggled, a hand slid between her legs, hard fingers pressing inside her. In spite of her terror, or perhaps partially because of it, her vaginal muscles contracted hard against the invasion, a gush of moisture opening and softening her.

The hands fell away as she was lifted and turned, forced to straddle bare, muscular thighs. The mattress bounced beside her, the second man apparently joining them on the bed. The man beneath her pulled her forward on his body, settling her so that the head of his huge cock pushed against her opening.

She screamed against her gag as she was lowered slowly but inexorably onto the hard shaft. She banged ineffectually against the man's broad chest with her fists, but he barely seemed to notice.

Her cunt spasmed involuntarily against its girth as the man's cock filled her. Still gripping her hips with strong fingers, he moved inside her, causing a convulsive shudder of pleasure to hurtle through her body.

Meanwhile, the second man repositioned himself just behind her on the bed. His breath was hot against her neck as he pushed a lubricated finger deep into her ass. Shea squealed against her gag, drool splashing down her chin, her heart thudding like a drum.

The finger was withdrawn, only to be replaced by the unmistakable pressure of a man's cock against her sphincter. He entered her ass slowly as the first man continued to pummel her cunt. The two cocks rubbed against each other inside her, separated only by a thin membrane, filling her completely, the sensation at once almost painful and deliciously pleasurable.

They began to move in tandem, Shea trapped between them, her body shuddering with each incredible dual thrust. She was so wet her inner thighs were slicked with her own juices as the supine man's pubic bone rubbed hard against her clit. Someone twisted her nipples, the added zing of erotic pain heightened by a hand gripping her hard just beneath the jaw.

She couldn't help it. It was going to happen, with or without permission.

Tuned to her body, the man behind her unbuckled the gag, while the man beneath her pulled the gooey ball from her mouth. She understood what was expected of her, and as the pleasure became nearly unbearable, she managed to gasp out the words.

"Please, Sir Stephen. Oh God, Master Zach. May I come?"

Shea opened her eyes, for a moment disoriented. She lay on her back in the hotel bed, Zach on one side, Steve on the other. They were both facing her. Zach was lifted on one elbow, his hand resting lightly on her breast, Steve with his head next to hers on the pillow.

"Hey there," Steve said with a smile. "You drifted off for a minute. You okay? How did we do with bringing one of your fantasies to life?"

Shea smiled and shook her head with wonder. "That was one of the most intense, scary, fabulous experiences of my life."

"When did you figure out it was us?" Zach asked, stroking her breast.

"I think I knew right away," Shea replied honestly. "But at the same time, I didn't, you know? I mean, I was *pretty* sure. But there was a part of me that couldn't believe it was happening. It told me you guys were back in Portland, and two strangers were here in the room with me, taking me, claiming me..." She hugged herself, a pleasurable shiver of fear moving through her.

"So it was good?" Steve queried. "Not *too* intense?"

"It was perfect," Shea breathed. "And once Zach had me on top of him, and I felt you behind me, I knew for sure it was my guys. I knew I was being claimed by my two Masters, the two men I love."

"And we love you," Zach murmured, pressing his palm over her heart.

Steve placed his hand over Zach's. "Yes, we do."

CONNECT WITH CLAIRE

Newsletter: http://tinyurl.com/o6tu4eu

Website: http://clairethompson.net

Romance Unbound Publishing: http://romanceunbound.com

Twitter: http://twitter.com/CThompsonAuthor

Facebook: http://www.facebook.com/ClaireThompsonauthor

Love Claire's work? Help spread the word for this indie author! Sign up for Claire's Advance Review Team. Email Claire at claire@clairethompson.net with your interest.

Manufactured by Amazon.ca
Bolton, ON